Safety First

"What about that friend of yours, Ed Triedle? Are you speakin' for him when you say that?"

"I don't know everything he does."

"So they weren't honest games?"

Slocum started to speak in his defense, but had to bite his tongue while ducking under the iron hook that sliced through the air on its way to his temple. While he was down there, he thumped a few quick punches into the butcher's stomach. Although the man's gut was thick and round, Slocum's knuckles bounced off what must have been mostly muscle. He stepped to one side and twisted his body around to avoid a downward blow from the meat hook.

Since the butcher had left himself completely open by missing that swing, Slocum had a choice to make. He could either draw his Colt and put the big man down for good or he could take his chances by trading a few more punches with the man. Whichever he decided on, Slocum knew he had to pick quickly if he was going to get out of town without a hook buried somewhere in his body.

JAKE LOGAN

SLOCUM
AND THE GHOST
OF ADAM WEYLAND

JOVE BOOKS, NEW YORK

WESTERN
LOG

THE BERKLEY PUBLISHING GROUP
Published by the Penguin Group
Penguin Group (USA) Inc.
375 Hudson Street, New York, New York 10014, USA
Penguin Group (Canada), 90 Eglinton Avenue East, Suite 700, Toronto, Ontario M4P 2Y3, Canada
(a division of Pearson Penguin Canada Inc.)
Penguin Books Ltd., 80 Strand, London WC2R 0RL, England
Penguin Group Ireland, 25 St. Stephen's Green, Dublin 2, Ireland (a division of Penguin Books Ltd.)
Penguin Group (Australia), 250 Camberwell Road, Camberwell, Victoria 3124, Australia
(a division of Pearson Australia Group Pty. Ltd.)
Penguin Books India Pvt. Ltd., 11 Community Centre, Panchsheel Park, New Delhi—110 017, India
Penguin Group (NZ), 67 Apollo Drive, Rosedale, North Shore 0632, New Zealand
(a division of Pearson New Zealand Ltd.)
Penguin Books (South Africa) (Pty.) Ltd., 24 Sturdee Avenue, Rosebank, Johannesburg 2196,
South Africa

Penguin Books Ltd., Registered Offices: 80 Strand, London WC2R 0RL, England

This is a work of fiction. Names, characters, places, and incidents either are the product of the author's imagination or are used fictitiously, and any resemblance to actual persons, living or dead, business establishments, events, or locales is entirely coincidental.

SLOCUM AND THE GHOST OF ADAM WEYLAND

A Jove Book / published by arrangement with the author

PRINTING HISTORY
Jove edition / May 2011

ISBN: 978-0-515-14937-1

JOVE®
Jove Books are published by The Berkley Publishing Group,
a division of Penguin Group (USA) Inc.
375 Hudson Street, New York, New York 10014.
JOVE® is a registered trademark of Penguin Group (USA) Inc.
The "J" design is a trademark of Penguin Group (USA) Inc.

PRINTED IN THE UNITED STATES OF AMERICA

10 9 8 7 6 5 4 3 2 1

1

BICKELL, TEXAS

Slocum's latest ride had taken him from New Mexico and was supposed to go all the way through Texas into Louisiana. It was a simple courier run to deliver some rich man's documents into New Orleans. Actually, Jerry Dawes might not have been rich, but that didn't stop him from looking down his nose at damn near everyone. From what Slocum had gleaned during his short time in Jerry's company, even his family didn't exactly feel blessed to spend time with the prick. Dawes was short-tempered, self-centered, and arrogant even though he didn't have the sense God gave a mule. That made Slocum more than ready to accept the job that was offered just so he could take that man's money and ride the hell away.

After two days, he'd found himself in Bickell. The Dusty Rose Saloon was the first watering hole to catch his attention, so Slocum stopped there for a spell to throw back some whiskey. Just when he'd been about to tip his hat, pay what he owed, and move on, someone shouted at him from across the room.

"Hey, stranger!"

Slocum ignored the loud greeting, having had his fill of blustering idiots back at the Dawes place.

"Hey, asshole! I'm talking to you."

Unwilling to let that one slide, Slocum turned around to face the table at the opposite side of the room. Although the men at that table were as far away as they could get from the bar, the cramped space of the Dusty Rose's interior didn't put them out of pistol range. Slocum lowered his hand to rest upon the grip of his holstered Colt Navy and asked, "You sure you're talking to me?"

"Yeah! You deaf?"

"No. Just impatient. I've also got business to tend to, so if you ease back on the smart lip, I can get back to it before you wind up on the floor with your head cracked open."

There were three men sitting at that table, two of which barely looked old enough to be drinking liquor instead of sarsaparilla. The third was about Slocum's age. At his table, he was the elder spokesman. After seeing the deadly promise in Slocum's eyes, however, he quickly changed his tune to one with a little less fire.

"No need for all of that, friend," the spokesman said. "I just had to catch your attention before you walked out that door."

Walking across the room to stop a few paces from the other man's table, Slocum said, "You've got it. Now what?"

"Now you can sit down and join us. That is," he added with a smirk, "if you'd grace us with your dignified presence."

Although the man was definitely a smart-ass, Slocum didn't think he was a dangerous one. "What's your name?"

"Ed Triedle. And you?"

Since he couldn't be completely sure about any of the men, Slocum decided not to gamble on one of them recognizing his name from a number of possible stories spreading across Texas. Some of those tales could earn him several rounds of free drinks in the Dusty Rose, but others might send a whole mess of hot lead flying in his direction. Hoping to avoid all of that, he simply replied, "I'm John."

That was good enough for Triedle, who kicked an empty chair a few inches away from the table. "Have a seat, John. You know how to play poker?"

"I may have dabbled."

"A dabbler, huh? Sounds like just the man we've been looking for. Poker just ain't as good with less than four in a game."

"Then why'd you start one up shorthanded?"

"Because the last man to sit in that chair lost a few hands and went home cryin' to Momma," Triedle replied. "Something tells me you're not that sort of fella."

The two younger men at the table sat with their eyes wide open and perched upon the edge of their seats as if they were ready to jump out of them at any moment. Triedle was another story. He was too loud to be taken completely seriously but too confident to be discarded. The gun at his hip was in a holster that looked as if it had seen some use, but there was no way for Slocum to be certain if Triedle had been the one doing the shooting or had simply won it off a more experienced fighter.

Under normal circumstances, Slocum might very well have tipped his hat and walked away from that offer just as he'd been ready to walk away from the bar. Jerry Dawes would have wanted him to put his nose to the grindstone and get back to the task for which he'd been paid. When Slocum thought of getting paid, his eyes were drawn immediately to the stacks of money in front of the three men at that table. There was enough there to double or even triple the fee Dawes was offering.

"So what do you say, John?" Triedle asked.

"I say you're absolutely right. Poker ain't any fun unless

you got four men at the table." With that, Slocum settled into his chair and dug into his pockets. "How much to buy in?"

A few hours later, Slocum was sitting behind a stack of cash that was four times bigger than the one he'd started with. Triedle drank like a fish and never got cross when he lost. Granted, he didn't lose very often compared to the two younger men at the table. Those boys kept their mouths shut and their eyes on their cards, which didn't help them in the slightest. Like most men their age, they had the fire in their bellies, but not enough experience to make anything burn.

"What've you got?" the one with the younger features of the two asked impatiently.

Slocum laid down three fours, a deuce, and the ace of clubs. Knowing the kid didn't have him beat, he could only sit there and try not to chuckle as the younger man stared daggers at the cards.

"You ain't gonna change 'em that way," Triedle said. "Just show or fold. Ain't no shame in admitting you're beat."

The kid threw his cards onto the table and shoved his chair back far enough to stand up.

"You gonna pitch a fit?" Triedle snapped.

The kid's mouth twitched, but he couldn't collect his thoughts well enough to put them into words. When he lowered his hand to within an inch of his gun, Slocum cocked his head and narrowed his eyes to glare at him.

"We've all lost a few hands, kid," he warned. "Take it like a man."

"I'm a man all right," the kid said. "Don't you worry about that. Did the two of you arrange this?"

"I beg your pardon?" Triedle asked.

The kid snapped half a glance toward Triedle's side of the table, but preferred to keep his gaze locked on Slocum. "You heard me, Ed. I think maybe you set it up for this stranger to come along so you could soak me and Nate here for all we got."

"I don't need any help with that," Triedle replied. "All I needed was a fourth to sit down so you'd stop whining about there not being enough at the table."

Slocum watched the kid carefully. He was definitely inexperienced with that weapon. As the kid's hand drifted closer to his gun, he looked more and more like he was lowering his britches in front of a woman for the first time. And right when it seemed things were about to cool down, Nate decided to stand up and throw in his two cents. "What've you got to say, Ed?" he asked. "Were you setting us up or not?"

Ed's response was short and sweet. "Nope."

"That good enough for ya?" Slocum asked. "Or should we make this into something bigger?"

The kid may have been young and inexperienced, but he knew when he was in over his head. Even so, he wasn't anxious to back down in front of his friend. Slocum gave him an out by leaning back and saying, "Have a seat and relax. Drinks are on me. After another hour, if you seriously think we're setting you up, I'll give your money back."

Reluctantly, the kid agreed. By the time the hour was up, he was too busy laughing at Triedle's jokes and enjoying his free drinks to notice he'd contributed even more to Slocum's chip stack.

The four of them agreed to meet for a game the following day. Slocum wasn't in any rush to get to New Orleans. Rather than oblige an asshole like Jerry Dawes, he rented a room at the Dusty Rose and played the next day's game. The day after that, more people threw in their ante to join the game until it grew into a genuine event. A rancher passing through town recognized Slocum, but that only added to the game's popularity.

Thanks to a few good hands and some more free drinks,

Slocum found himself with some serious cash in his pockets. If Jerry Dawes found out about all the time spent dawdling in Bickell, he would have thrown a fit worse than the kid's.

That made Slocum grin.

When he came downstairs on his third day in town, the Dusty Rose was busier than ever. Even though there were still a few empty seats to be found, the barkeep couldn't have been happier. He was a squat man who looked as if he'd been carved from a pile of beef with a dull cleaver. There was no real definition to his lumpy body and his skin was tanned to the color of old leather. According to the look on the barkeep's face, seeing Slocum come down from his room was akin to seeing a bag of money delivered to his doorstep.

"Mornin', Mister Slocum! Got quite a crowd for your game today."

"Mornin', Harry. Since when did it become my game?"

The barkeep shrugged, wiped off some spilt beer in front of him, and asked, "Set you up with a round of drinks for the players like always?"

"Ah," Slocum mused. "So that's why it's my game."

His first instinct was to save some cash and decline the offer. Then again, since most of the men already playing had proven to loosen their purse strings after a few splashes of whiskey hit the backs of their throats, Slocum considered paying for those drinks to be a good investment.

"Sure," he said, which was enough to make Harry's face light up brighter than the noonday sun. "Set me up with two bottles, but no more than that. Anyone comes nosing around, you let them pay for their own damn drinks. I won't stand for what happened last night."

"Honest mistake," the barkeep said while raising both hands.

The incident in question came during a string of intense hands between Slocum and Triedle. During that time, a few of the observers got themselves drunk by telling the bar-keep that Slocum agreed to pay for them to do so. Those men eventually sat down to play, but Slocum wasn't about to take that gamble again.

"I'll take that first drink now, Harry."

"Sure thing, Mister Slocum," the barkeep replied while anxiously filling a small glass with his best whiskey.

Slocum downed the firewater, closed his eyes for a moment, and waited for the burn to kick in. As always, it started in his throat and rolled like a wave through his entire body straight down to his toes. When he opened his eyes again, everything in the room seemed to be brighter. "Nice stuff," he said while holding up the empty glass. "Everyone else gets what's in that bottle, though."

Harry didn't have to look to know that Slocum was pointing to a less expensive brand. His smile dimmed, but came back a little as he asked, "Another late night?"

"We'll see about that."

"Yeah," grunted another man a little farther along the bar. "We'll just see about that." He stood less than an inch shorter than Slocum with light blond hair and eyes that were blue enough to stand in stark contrast to his pale face. His clothes hung on him as if they'd been carelessly thrown over the back of a chair and his shoulders were only slightly less angular than a wooden frame. He gripped a tin cup overflowing with beer foam, and judging by the shakiness of his hand, it wasn't the first one he'd had that night. When he realized that Slocum had taken notice of him, he straightened up as if to accept a silent challenge. "What the hell you lookin' at?"

"Someone who needs to check where he points his damn mouth before he starts shooting it off."

"I know what I'm doin'."

Now that he'd heard the man slur a few sentences, Slocum was willing to let it pass. He wasn't one to put up with guff like that for no reason, but he had better things to occupy his time than knocking some idiot drunk on his ass.

Suddenly, the drunk slapped his hand flat upon the top of the bar and walked toward Slocum. "Who the hell are you?" he asked. "Some sort of big man? Let's see how big you are!"

The drunk's hand was anything but quick as it flapped against his holster in a fumbling attempt to draw what looked to be an old .44. Before the gun could see the light of day, Slocum leaned forward and dropped his hand on top of the drunk's to trap the pistol where it was. "Whatever you think I did to start this, you've got it wrong. Let it drop."

"That's right, Adam," the barkeep said. "Let it drop."

"I won't let nothin' drop!" the drunk bellowed. Even with his hand squashed between Slocum's palm and the grip of his own pistol, he continued to try and pull it loose. Slocum responded by applying even more pressure until the drunk's fingers crunched around the pistol's grip. He then forced that hand up and twisted it against the joint.

"How about now?" he asked calmly.

The drunk stared at Slocum, but was obviously having a hard time keeping his chin up. Since he'd been getting a lot of practice in letting idiots save face, Slocum took one of the bottles he'd bought and poured enough whiskey into Adam's glass to top it off. "There you go," he said. "Better?"

"I s'pose."

"If you feel like making some easy money, head on over to our game. Lining your pockets with some of them boys' cash has been going a long ways in keeping a smile tacked onto my face."

"You hear that, Adam?" Harry said enthusiastically. "You can play some cards if you like."

Adam picked up his whiskey while Slocum delivered the rest to the card game. He sniffed it as though he suspected it had been poisoned and then drank it down.

2

It felt strange for Slocum to sit at a table in the Dusty Rose without having cards in his hands. Instead, he had a knife and fork so he could enjoy a meal of steak and potatoes that was given to him courtesy of the management. When he looked over to the bar, Harry waved as if he was greeting a long-lost relative. Too bad Slocum couldn't be so happy about the food.

"You should really try the place down the street," Triedle said as he sidled up to Slocum's table and took a chair from another one. "Much better food and the serving girls are a hell of a lot nicer than that one over there."

Although he seemed to know he was the topic of discussion, Harry must not have known the tone of Triedle's comments because his smile was wider than ever as he returned the gambler's wave.

"He's giving out free meals to those of us playing the game," Slocum said. "You might want to partake before he changes his mind."

"One poorly cooked slab of beef before you move along, huh?" When Slocum looked at him with a raised eyebrow,

Triedle added, "I figured you were headed out of town pretty soon."

"If you can read me that well, I'm surprised you didn't win more of my money."

"No science to it. A man just tends to play recklessly when he's ahead and intends on skipping out of town."

"I ain't skipping nowhere," Slocum said. "I got a job to do. Did you think I was sinking roots here?"

"Not hardly! Headed out to New Orleans?"

Before Slocum got too surprised about a fancy bit of fortune telling, he recalled talking about that during the previous night's game. "That's right."

"Is the pay for that job of yours enough to leave what you've got going here?"

Slocum chuckled while sawing into a particularly tough portion of his steak. "If you mean the game, I'd say it's about the right time to go. Those boys are out of money, the locals are getting tired of losing, and those two gamblers in the fancy suits that sat down at the table last night are getting ready to run something that will either end up with us losing our shirts or having to get our hands bloody when we catch them cheating."

Triedle nodded slowly. "You have a good eye, John. But the last few hands of a game like this is like wringing out a washcloth. Sometimes you're surprised how much water keeps trickling out."

"Yeah? Well, you can keep on wringing because I'm riding out of this town as soon as I'm done with this steak." When his teeth crunched down on a large hunk of gristle, he added, "Or maybe a little sooner."

"Would you be opposed to some company?"

"That depends. Do you mean you?"

"Actually, yes!"

"Then yes," Slocum said with a curt nod. "I would be opposed."

The disappointed look on Triedle's face was priceless. It

was short-lived, however, since his attention was quickly diverted to a woman with long, light brown hair who approached the table with her hands clasped in front of her.

"Pardon me," she said. "I hope I'm not interrupting."

Triedle was quick to get to his feet and remove his hat. "Not at all, ma'am. How can I be of assistance?"

"Are you John?"

"No, that'd be my good friend with the steak."

Slocum nodded and continued to saw off another hunk of beef. The steak smelled just good enough to keep going and he'd be damned if he would turn his nose up at a free meal.

"I'd like to thank you, then. My name's Mia Weyland." When that didn't get a reaction from him, she added, "I'm Adam Weyland's sister."

Still nothing.

"I hear that he gave you some trouble earlier," she said with confusion creeping into her pretty features.

"I believe she's referring to the gentleman over at the bar," Triedle explained.

Slocum looked over there while putting the pieces of the conversation together in his head. "Oh, you mean the drunk?"

Although she seemed uncomfortable with that description, she could hardly dispute it. "Yes. My brother has not been feeling well and has consequently been drinking rather heavily. I apologize if he caused you any trouble."

"Don't mention it," Slocum said.

Mia had kind eyes, round cheeks, and hair that fell in large curls that brushed against her forehead and neck. Soft, creamy skin made her look very much like a doll that had been propped up and sent over to Slocum's table. She separated her hands, shifted on her feet, and then laced her fingers together once again.

"John and I were just discussing traveling to New Orleans," Triedle announced.

"Is that a fact?" Mia asked. "I have family in Louisiana."

Suddenly, the prospect of leaving some of his free steak behind didn't seem so bad when compared to the slow-moving agony of the conversation. He pushed his plate away, shoved back from the table, and stood up. "Now that you mention it, I should get going to Louisiana right about now."

Both of the other two at the table seemed completely surprised by the fact that Slocum didn't want to swap any more meaningless words with them. Triedle stood up as if he were connected to him by a harness. "I had some business I wanted to discuss with you," he said.

"If that business has to do with coming to Louisiana, you're more than welcome to do that." Just when Triedle began to smile, Slocum added, "You can go wherever the hell you want to go, just not with me. I've got a schedule to uphold and you'd only slow me down."

"You don't know that!"

"Yeah, I think I do."

Since Slocum was already on his way to the door, Triedle followed him out.

No matter how quickly the gambler moved, Mia was even quicker. She got to Slocum just as he made it outside. "I have something I'd like to discuss with you as well," she said.

"Apology accepted on your brother's behalf," Slocum quickly said. "Don't think any more of it. You seem like a nice lady and your brother seems like a loud drunk. I'm sure you've got plenty of other folks to apologize to, so I'll let you get to it."

Outside, the street was busier than normal. Horses were tied to several nearby posts, allowing their owners to spend time inside the Dusty Rose as well as a number of other establishments in the vicinity. Slocum found his horse right away, since he'd brought it out of the stable earlier that morning in preparation for a hasty departure.

"Mister Slocum?" Mia called out behind him.

He walked to his horse and started tugging at the reins to get them loosened from where they'd been tied. His hands moved even quicker when the others strode to catch up to him. If he could only work fast enough, he might somehow get away without answering to either one of them.

"Get your hands off'a me, you son of a bitch!"

Slocum had been so intent on the distractions behind him that the outburst in front of him had gone completely unnoticed until those words exploded through the air. They came from a small crowd gathered in the middle of the street a little ways down from the Dusty Rose Saloon. As Slocum looked that way, the part of him that wanted to move along was still screaming in the back of his mind for him to do just that. And like so many other times in his life, he ignored it.

"What the hell is that about?" he muttered, mostly to himself.

Mia was close enough to hear him and replied in a worried tone, "That's probably what I wanted to talk to you about."

There was scuffling in the middle of the crowd, followed by the distinct crack of knuckles against flesh. When he heard a woman scream and a bunch of men begin to shout, Slocum rushed toward the commotion. By the time he'd shoved through enough of the crowd to get a look at the middle of it, Slocum was in the perfect spot to catch an elbow to the chin as a big fellow cocked an arm back to take a swing at someone else. The blow landed solidly on his mouth, staggering Slocum and almost knocking him down. Thankfully, an overly curious old man was positioned to break his fall.

"Damn, it," grunted the big fellow who'd cracked Slocum. "See what you made me do? Someone hold that drunk up so he can get what's comin' to him!"

After clearing the fog from his head, Slocum was able to

see Adam Weyland standing proudly in the middle of the ruckus. His face was already bloody and his clothes were rumpled to the point where they seemed to have been almost twisted completely around in the wrong direction on his lanky frame. "I know what's comin' to me!" he said in a voice that reeked of whiskey and every other kind of liquor sold in the county. "Just like I knew what was comin' to your wife last night. And your sister!"

The man who'd accidentally elbowed Slocum rushed at Adam like a bull. If the drunkard had had any wits about him, he could have cleared a path so the charge would have landed on one of the three men behind him. Instead, Adam caught the brunt of a straight punch to the face that snapped his head back and sent a spray of blood through the air. The crowd gasped and Adam stumbled backward. Amazingly enough, he remained upright instead of dropping to the ground, where he seemed to belong.

When he looked back to the man who'd punched him, Adam was smiling. "That all you got?" he asked through blood-smeared teeth. "No wonder your wife was so anxious to drop her britches for me."

The second punch was harder than the first and had no trouble whatsoever in sending Adam to the ground. He landed solidly with his legs splayed and his head drooping forward. Adam mumbled something after spitting out a wad of crimson juice. Although Slocum couldn't hear what was said, the man who'd dropped Adam like a bad habit heard it just fine.

"Stand back," the angry fellow said. As soon as the other men moved away from Adam, the fellow drove his boot into the drunk's chin with so much force that Slocum wouldn't have been surprised to see Adam's head sail through the air. Instead, the drunk continued to laugh as he toppled over sideways and absorbed the first of many kicks to his ribs.

As the beating became more intense, the crowd closed in around the spectacle like a bunch of piranhas that had discovered a chunk of raw meat floating in their lake. Slocum pushed his way through until he could reach out and grab the angry fellow's shoulder and pull him back.

"Let go of me," the angry fellow said as he wheeled around to look directly at Slocum's battered face. "Who the hell are you?"

"What happened here?"

Obviously not concerned enough by his first question to follow it up, the fellow replied, "He slapped my wife on the ass and called her a whore."

Slocum looked at Adam and only got a hacking laugh in return.

"Then he soiled the name of my sister."

"Yeah," Slocum sighed. "I heard that part."

"Why the hell would you want to step in on this ass-hole's behalf?"

Rather than admit to thinking the same question himself, Slocum asked, "Did he do anything other than that?"

"I don't think so."

"Then he doesn't deserve to die just for talking. As for the slap, I'd say he got what was coming to him and then some."

The crowd parted once more, allowing Mia to make her way to her brother's side. For the first time since the beating had started, Adam looked like he wasn't happy with the direction his life had taken. "Aw, no!" he groused. "Mia, just get away from me."

Despite his struggles, she took hold of his arm and pulled him up. Adam fought her every step of the way, kicking and flailing even as he was set onto his own two feet. "You're coming with me," she said. "Before you get yourself hurt."

"He's already hurt," the angry fellow said. "And it's about to get a whole lot worse."

That was all the other men in the crowd needed to hear. They closed in around Adam and pulled Mia away so the fellow who balled up a fist could slam it into Adam's face.

Once more, Adam accepted the blow as if he'd ordered it off a menu.

Grabbing the angry fellow's arm, Slocum said, "That's enough!"

"Are you sticking your neck out for this piece of shit?"

"No more than I would for anyone else. This has gone far enough. Why don't we put a stop to this before the law gets here to cart us all to jail?"

"No need to worry about that."

"How can you be so sure?"

The angry fellow responded to that by pulling aside the flap of his vest to reveal a tin star pinned to the shirt he wore beneath it. While Slocum struggled for what he should say next, Mia pried her brother away from the hands of the men who kept him upright.

"So just because he said some bad things, he's going to be beaten to death in the street like an animal?" she asked.

Every second that passed without him striking Adam caused the angry lawman to lose some of the fire in his eyes. Finally, he looked more like someone who'd woken up to find himself in a strange bed without any recollection of how he'd landed there. "You're right, ma'am," he said.

Mia spun around to examine her brother and fuss with his rumpled clothes. "Of course I'm right," she said.

The whole crowd seemed to let go of a deep breath. Slocum wasn't sure what he meant to do when he'd waded into that mess, but was sure he wouldn't have resolved anything that quickly. Leave it to a pretty lady to cut straight through to the heart of trouble and set it straight.

Apparently, Mia was just as surprised with how well things seemed to be going. "Well then," she said, "we'll just be on our way. I apologize on my brother's behalf."

The lawman nodded, waited for her to take a few steps away, and then snapped a sharp punch directly into Adam's eye. The drunk staggered back a few steps, leaving Mia speechless and the lawman rubbing his reddened knuckles.

"That's for what you said about my sister," he said. "Now get the hell outta my sight before I fix it so you can't open your mouth again."

Slocum moved past the lawman. He couldn't believe Adam was still on his feet by the time he got to him. Judging by the welts, cuts, and bruises on his face, it seemed to be a small miracle that he was even conscious at all. Despite the vacant grin on his face, Adam was feeling no pain. The stench of liquor at such a close range was bad enough to make Slocum feel as if he'd just helped himself to a quick shot of whiskey.

"All right, everyone," the lawman bellowed. "Move along. Can't you see there are wagons that want to get by? Step aside and let 'em pass."

Deprived of their show, the crowd lost interest in Adam Weyland, his sister, Slocum, and even the lawman who'd done his best to knock Adam into oblivion. Slocum couldn't tell if the other men who'd swarmed in on the lawman's behalf were deputies or just locals eager to get closer to the spectacle because they'd wandered off as well. Even so, Slocum wasn't going to count his blessings until he, Adam, and Mia all made it to the boardwalk.

"Now what in blazes was *that* about?" Mia snarled, beating Slocum to the punch.

Adam shook his head and tried to push her aside so he could stagger away, but didn't make it far before Slocum snagged him by the elbow and pulled him back. "She saved your useless life," he said to the drunkard. "The least you can do is answer her."

But Adam didn't have time for either of them. He swatted at Slocum and Mia as if they were gnats pestering him on a hot summer day.

"What did you do now?" Mia asked. When her brother muttered something and spun away from her, she dashed around to get in front of him. "Talk to me! What's wrong with you? Are you trying to get yourself killed? Isn't it bad enough that you wound up in jail the last time you pulled this kind of nonsense?"

"Leave me alone!"

"I can't leave you alone. You're my brother."

"Just get away from me, bitch!"

Slocum strode up to Adam, turned him around, and thumped a solid punch into his gut. The impact doubled Adam over and dropped him to his knees. Before he could fall, a small crowd of bloodthirsty locals took notice and began to circle the three of them.

"Go on," Slocum said as he took off his hat and swatted at one of the closest onlookers. "Mind yer own business, you bunch of vultures!"

Since all there was to look at was a drunk, a woman who now wiped at the tears forming in her eyes, and an angry man waving a hat, the crowd dispersed.

"Are you going to come home with me or should I let the sheriff toss you into a cell?" Mia asked.

Adam grumbled incoherently, but decided to stagger along beside her as she walked away from the Dusty Rose. He lost his footing for a moment, fell forward, and almost knocked a big man in a butcher's apron into the street. The big man wheeled around and warned, "Watch where you're goin'."

"Or what, you fat piece of shit?" Adam snapped.

The butcher wasn't about to wait for Mia, Slocum, or anyone else to stand in front of him before taking a swing at the drunk. A fist the size of a boiled ham pounded against the side of Adam's face with enough force to knock him straight to the wooden slats under his feet. Slocum was content to let the drunk idiot lie there and get what was coming to him until Mia rushed over to put herself between the butcher's fists and her brother's face.

"Aw, hell," Slocum growled and dove into yet another fray. When the butcher's knuckles smashed into his jaw, he hoped he only lost one tooth instead of all of them.

By some miracle, Adam still wasn't knocked out. He reached around Slocum's body and jabbed the butcher with a few quick punches. Even though the chopping blows didn't do much in the way of damage, they sure stoked the fire that had brought the butcher this far. To make matters worse, Adam's last punch had come in at just the right angle to make it seem as if the punch had been thrown by Slocum. The big man pulled himself up to his full height and glared down at Slocum while asking, "You just hit me?"

"No," Slocum replied. "This is all just a big mistake."

For a moment, it seemed that was enough to cool the butcher down. He cocked his head to one side and said, "I think I know you."

"Really? That's nice. How about we all just shake hands and be on our way?"

"Yeah. I do know you. You're the man who cheated my brother Nate out of all that money in a card game."

"Nate?"

The butcher nodded. "You know who I'm talkin' about and you're sure as hell the man who cheated him."

Forgetting all about Adam in the time it took for the butcher to reach for the meat hook that had been looped over his apron string, Slocum said, "I didn't cheat anyone. Those were all fair games."

"What about that friend of yours, Ed Triedle? Are you speakin' for him when you say that?"

"I don't know everything he does."

"So they weren't honest games?"

Slocum started to speak in his defense, but had to bite his tongue while ducking under the iron hook that sliced through the air on its way to his temple. While he was down there, he thumped a few quick punches into the butcher's stomach. Although the man's gut was thick and round, Slocum's knuckles bounced off what must have been mostly muscle. He stepped to one side and twisted his body around to avoid a downward blow from the meat hook.

Since the butcher had left himself completely open by missing that swing, Slocum had a choice to make. He could either draw his Colt and put the big man down for good or he could take his chances by trading a few more punches with the man. Whichever he decided on, Slocum knew he had to pick quickly if he was going to get out of town without a hook buried somewhere in his body.

3

Slocum rode east along the trail out of Bickell. Every part of his body hurt. His clothes were filthy with dried blood and his face was swollen on one side. Even the subtle movements of shifting in his saddle sent waves of pain through him.

"Why the hell didn't you just shoot that big bastard?" Triedle asked.

Looking over to the man who rode beside him was enough to send a jolt through Slocum's neck, all the way down to the portions of his shoulder and chest that had been pummeled by the butcher's fists. "And why didn't you step in to help me when that bastard refused to drop?"

Triedle shrugged and wrapped the reins around his fist. "Thought you knew what you were doing."

"That man was after you and the only reason he didn't take your head off was because he couldn't get through me."

"For which I already thanked you. In case you missed it those other times," Triedle said while tapping his finger against the brim of his hat, "thank you again."

"Why are you still in my sight?"

21

"Because we're both headed to New Orleans and we make a hell of a good team at the card table. Do you even know how many big poker games are played in New Orleans every night?"

"Don't care," Slocum replied.

"Lots. Dozens. Maybe hundreds. Well, hundreds may be an exaggeration. Then again, it may not be. Either way, we could stand to make plenty in just a few days."

"I'm not going there to play poker. I've got a job to do."

"Right," Triedle said. "That the same job you were talking about the first night you were in Bickell? The one given to you by that smug piece of work with the sweet little wife?" Slocum didn't answer, but that didn't slow Triedle down in the slightest. "If you were so concerned about that job, you wouldn't have stayed in Bickell so long in the first place. I recognize something in you, John. Once you get a whiff of the money that's to be made in New Orleans, you won't be so quick to leave."

"I've seen New Orleans."

"Not with me as your guide!"

Slocum sighed and turned to look at the people riding to his left. For most of the day, Mia had been busy tending to her brother. That was a difficult enough task considering they were riding on two horses moving side by side, but Adam wasn't making her job any easier by fretting like a little boy who didn't want to put on his church clothes. He muttered and grumbled and would have done a better job of squirming away from her if every one of his actions wasn't accompanied by the pained grimace of a man just coming out of a drunken stupor.

"Just because this idiot insists on hitching his wagon to me doesn't mean you have to do the same," Slocum told her.

Mia smiled and tucked away the handkerchief she'd been using to dab at her brother's cheek. "We won't trouble you for long. It just seemed like a good idea for all of us to get away when we had the chance."

"You mean when that butcher stopped beating his ass," Adam said.

Twisting in his saddle, Slocum faced the recovering drunk and said, "I put him down long enough for you to walk away unscathed, in case you forgot."

"Unscathed?" Adam jabbed a finger at a nasty cut running the length of his left cheek and asked, "You call this unscathed?"

"I'd call that lucky considering how many folks in town wanted to do a hell of a lot worse!"

Triedle laughed under his breath. "No wonder his sister was so quick to get out when she had some protection." When Mia glared at him, he added, "I'm just stating the obvious! The way that brother of yours has been shooting his mouth off, you wouldn't have made it more than a few feet before someone walked up and blew his head off. Since John here knocked that butcher out with a little help from a frying pan . . ."

"That was a horseshoe," Slocum corrected. "It was on the ground and I put it to use."

Adam stood up halfway in his stirrups before Mia reached over to tug on his arm. It didn't take much effort on her part to ease him back down, but he winced and grumbled as though she'd forcibly thrown him into his seat.

"You're right," she said. "We needed to get away from that town before someone killed my brother. It wouldn't have been much longer before he was either shot or beaten so badly that he might as well be dead." When Adam grumbled something Slocum couldn't make out, she was quick to scold him into silence. Locking eyes with Slocum, she asked, "Is it all right if we ride with you for a while?"

"How long? I've got some time to make up."

"Right," Triedle said. "Wouldn't want to fall off your precious schedule."

Not responding to that comment, Mia said, "Just until we cross the Louisiana border. Like I said, we've got family there."

"We left town in a rush," Slocum said. "Are you ready for a ride like this?"

She winced slightly and then put a shaky smile on top of it. "Well, our place is a little farther down this trail. If we could make a little diversion, I could pick up a few things. Just some clothes and such. I can also get some of the money I've been pulling together to help with expenses and the like. It's not a lot, but it should be enough to put us up in some hotels or pay for supplies and food."

"Or a fee for our troubles," Triedle was quick to offer. "Since you were so anxious to hitch your wagon to John and me, I'm assuming you don't want to make this excursion on your own."

Reluctantly, she nodded. "That's right. My brother needs to get out of town, and in his condition, he won't be much use to me along the way. In fact, he might be a hindrance."

"Just like I've always been!" Adam bellowed. "Is that what you mean to say? 'Cause if it is, you should just say it!"

"Yes," she spat angrily. "Just like you've always been. Are you satisfied?"

"Yeah."

"Good. Since you've uprooted us once more just when it seemed like we'd found a place to live in peace. I hope you are happy. Maybe you'll be happier back in Louisiana."

"You know what would make me happier?" Adam asked.

"Yes I do, but I won't let that happen. Not after all we've been through to make it this far." Taking a deep breath to calm herself, she turned toward Slocum as if there was the slightest chance that he hadn't been privy to the dustup between her and Adam. "Ed's right. I don't want to make the trip on my own, and as you can see, even if my brother is with me, I'd still be on my own. If you could help us get to Louisiana, I'd be willing to pay. You could put that money to use however you see fit and keep a fair percentage as a fee for your services. All I ask is that we get to where we're going without too much hardship along the way."

"Not used to sleeping under the stars?" Slocum asked.

She showed him a genuine smile this time. "It's been a while."

"If I'm such a burden," Adam said, "then maybe you should leave me behind. Or just knock me off 'a my horse to rot somewhere along the side of the trail. That'll suit me just fine!"

"I'm sure it would," she said in a tired, exasperated voice. "But you're my brother and you'll stay with me."

"You don't think I can be trusted with yer new goddamn friends?"

"It's not that, Adam. I just don't think anyone else but me would be able to choke back the urge to knock you on your ass and leave you wherever you land. Since I've already gone through too much and sacrificed too many years of my life to keep you above ground, you're staying with me. Is that all right with you, Mister Slocum?"

"That's more than all right with me, ma'am."

"Please," she chuckled. "It's bad enough that I have to act like my mother around Adam. I'd rather not be addressed as such by a man like you. Call me Mia."

"Then you'll call me John. Fair's fair."

"Right," Triedle chimed in. "We're all just one big group traveling together. Partners, even!"

"Don't push it, Ed," Slocum warned. "I haven't agreed to anything like that with you. Far as I'm concerned, you're just someone that's taking up the same stretch of trail as me. There's always plenty for me to do to rectify that situation."

Triedle kept his mouth shut as Mia stifled a laugh at his expense.

"Don't feel too good to be smacked down like a dog, does it?" Adam asked. "But judging by the condition of John's face, I'd say he already knows all about that."

"You've got a concerned sister riding with you," Slocum told him. "But it's a long way to New Orleans and there'll be plenty of chances for me to finish the job that was started by all those men who drove you out of Bickell."

The menace in Slocum's tone shut Adam's mouth for the time being. When he saw his sister point her horse's nose to the south and snap her reins, he was quick to follow. She rode at a pace that steadily grew faster despite Adam's loud petitions for her to slow down. Even after all that complaining, he managed to catch up and match her pace before she got too far ahead of him.

"So," Triedle said as he rode beside Slocum, "you think we'll see them again?"

"Doesn't matter if we do or don't. I'm headed to New Orleans either way."

"You mean *we're* headed to New Orleans."

"Whatever you say."

"Do you disagree with that?"

Casting only a fleeting glance in Triedle's direction, Slocum asked, "Did I ever say anything to make you think otherwise?"

"We could make a hell of a lot of money, you and I."

"So you keep saying."

"Tell you what. There are plenty of saloons between here and Louisiana. Texas is full of cattle barons, cowboys, and ranchers who love their cards and are plenty eager to get a good game started up. Why don't we see firsthand how well we work together? Personally, I think we've already proven that point, but if you need some more convincing . . ."

Slocum's attention was still fixed upon Mia and Adam's silhouettes as they slowly dwindled to the south. The two horses had taken a steady course, but Adam's wild gesturing could be seen even from a distance. Whatever he was saying to his sister, he was giving her hell with both barrels.

"I'm not trying to swindle you, if that's what you think," Triedle continued. "It's just a mutually beneficial business arrangement. Why did you even agree to deliver this package or letter or whatever it is you agreed to carry for that Jerry fellow?"

"To get the hell away from him, shut his mouth, and take some of his money to boot."

Triedle laughed and said, "So you were listening to me after all, huh?"

"Doesn't seem like I have much choice."

"You do with that one." When Slocum looked over at him, Triedle added, "You could make sure they don't catch up to us by taking any number of other routes into Louisiana. For that matter, you could just put the spurs to that horse of yours so that lady and her squawking brother don't even find a dust trail."

"I could. Of course, I could do the same to you. All I need is a head start and something heavy enough for me to give you the same medicine I gave to that butcher."

"You wouldn't damage the man who can make you rich!" Although the expression on Slocum's face wasn't very promising, Triedle was confident enough to look away from him and to the two horses that were cresting a ridge to the south. "Adam Weyland is nothing but trouble. He welcomes it."

"Yeah. I know."

"We'd be better off without them."

Slocum glared at him and snapped his reins.

4

There were three houses clustered together less than four miles outside of Bickell. Each sat upon a square of land belonging to a family and was fenced in to make each piece of property look more like a picture that had been situated perfectly on its patch of ground beneath a wide open Texas sky. When Mia got close enough to see her house in between the other two, she pulled back on her reins. Her brother did the same and asked, "What's the matter?"

"You're not slurring your words for a change. Did that ride sober you up?"

"I suppose so," he grunted. "You expect to hear how grateful I am to you for taking me under your precious wing or should we just get what we came for?"

"You never miss a chance to dig at me," she said. "Drunk or sober, you never let one opportunity slip by."

"I'm through telling you I'm sorry, Mia. If you stopped to hear me say that, then forget it. I'm through saying them words to anyone."

She looked at him with an expression that began as stern and then drifted into exasperated. When she lost the ability

28

to maintain that, she turned away before he could see what came next. "That's not why I stopped. Do you recognize those men on the Samsons' porch?"

Adam shot a quick glance toward the houses and shook his head. "What are you talking about? I can't see anything from here."

"Look again."

After a few moments, he shook his head and started to fret as if he meant to throw himself off his horse's back. "This is ridiculous. Are we gonna fetch the money and go or are we gonna sit here looking at the damn neighbors?"

"Will and Agnes Samson are older than the hills and don't have any children left. Take a look at those men and tell me they belong there."

Adam looked again, but truly took the time to observe instead of simply pointing his eyes in a direction and holding them there. That little bit of effort was all it took to give him pause. "Neither one of those fellas looks like Will Samson, that's for certain. And they sure ain't Agnes."

"I'm glad you think this is funny. Those men have been on and off that porch for the last week."

"What're they doing there?"

"Waiting for you," she said. "That's what they told me."

Adam's expression darkened before he lowered his head and gripped his reins even tighter. "They told you that?"

"Yes they did."

"What else did they tell you?"

She maintained the straight posture that she'd had for the entire ride, but it required a lot more effort than before. "They said that if you didn't pay them what you owed, they'd take it out of your hide. Yours and mine."

Those last two words, more than any of the others, struck Adam like a fist in the stomach. He clenched his jaw and snarled, "We'll just see about that."

Grabbing on to his arm with enough force to keep him from moving away, Mia asked, "What do you owe those men? Is it money? I've got some money stashed away. It isn't much, but it should be enough to get you out of this mess. If that's what it takes, then I can pay it."

"That money was given to you for good reason. And you're right. It isn't much. It's yours, though. Not mine. That's how it should be."

"Are those the men you used to ride with? The ones from Amarillo?"

"Let go of me, Mia. This is my fight. Not yours."

"How much do you owe?" When she was unable to get her answer, she asked a different question. "Do you even know how much they want or were you too drunk to remember?"

"I know," he said through gritted teeth. "It's a lot."

"Oh my God. You don't know. What is the matter with you, Adam? Ever since you were told that—"

He pulled away from her as if he were breaking an iron grip and almost pulled them both from their saddles in the process. "I'm through with saying I'm sorry and I'm through with listening to lectures. That should save us both some trouble."

"You don't even know what you owe those men," she said. "What do you intend on doing to appease them now? Talk to them? The only thing you've been able to talk yourself into anymore is a beating."

"Maybe that's what I need."

"Maybe it is! But if you haven't had any sense beaten into you yet, then I don't know how much good it's going to do now."

"And what good do you intend on doing?" he asked. "You think throwing me onto the back of a horse and dragging my sorry hide all the way to that shack in the Louisiana swamp is going to cure what ails me? Ain't nothing in Louisiana can do that and you know it."

"You've always been good to me, Adam. These last several months notwithstanding, you've always been a good brother. Can you keep that up for just a little while longer? As a favor to me? If we get far enough away from Amarillo, maybe this will all just blow over."

Adam's face remained twisted into an ugly scowl, but his eyes showed a hint of softening around the edges. A subtle twitch in one cheek made it even more apparent that he was struggling to keep his stern façade in place. No matter what his eyes were saying, however, his mouth was quicker on the draw.

"I already owe you more favors than I could ever repay," he told her. "Tacking one more on to that won't do either of us any good."

"Maybe you don't know what's good for either of us right now. Maybe it's time you stopped charging blindly through your life and let someone guide you for a little while. Isn't that what family is for?"

"You've had the job for too long." Adam lowered his head, placed his hand to his mouth, and cleared his throat. Before too long, he started hacking with enough force to shake his shoulders and almost crumple him over in his saddle. Mia reached out to place a hand on his back, but he swatted it away before she could do the first bit of comforting.

When she looked at the houses again, all three porches were empty. "Adam, I think we should get what we came for."

He looked up as well and asked, "Where'd they go?"

"I don't care. Let's just pick up that money."

"I'd go get it for you, but you never told me where you stashed it."

"Can you blame me?" When her brother merely shrugged, she added, "Just come along with me and stay outside. I won't be a moment, so let me know if someone comes along."

"Someone's coming along," he said almost immediately.

Just as Mia was about to scold him for wasting time with bad jokes, she saw the horses galloping around the

Samson house. She couldn't be certain, but the men in the saddles looked an awful lot like the ones that had been sitting outside only a few moments ago. "Don't say a word," she said. "Maybe they're headed back to town."

There were three riders in all. One of them split off to the north and the other two came straight at Mia and Adam.

"There's another one coming up behind us," Adam said as he drew the old .44 that had been hanging at his side since his days in the Army.

"Put that gun away," Mia hissed. "You'll only start more trouble."

"Too late for that."

The first shot was announced by a sharp crack and a puff of smoke from one of the riders charging directly at the siblings. Having never been in the line of fire before, Mia was too shocked to even snap her reins. The bullet kicked up a mound of dirt a few yards away, which caused her horse to nervously sidestep from the point of impact.

"Son of a bitch!" Adam shouted while straightening his arm and sighting along the top of his pistol.

Both of the other horses fanned out and came to a halt. The third had circled around to Adam's right. "We're just after the money you owe us," shouted the rider who'd already pulled his trigger. "That was a warning shot. Unless you settle your debt, the next one will hurt a whole lot more."

"You want me, Paul? Come and get me!" Adam replied while squinting at the men in front of him. "Just leave my sister out of it."

Mia took in the scene with wide eyes, twisting around in her saddle to see as much of what was happening as she could. That movement, along with the shot that had already been fired, caused her horse to fidget from one hoof to another. She spotted a fourth rider behind them. He was a little farther away than the other three and was sitting like a statue to watch what was going on.

"Drop that shooting iron or we'll drop both of you!" Paul shouted back.

"You make one move in that direction and I'll make you pay for it!"

As much as she hated the direction the conversation was taking, Mia didn't know what to do about it. She wasn't experienced in gunfights, but she did know when she was in a bad spot and having armed men almost completely surrounding her was one of the worst she could imagine. Unfortunately, her brother seemed intent on making it even worse.

"You there as well, Cale?" Adam asked.

"You know I am."

"In that case, I'll talk to you up close like a man. Since you're too yellow to come within pistol range, I'll come to you." He rode toward the two men, either ignoring his sister's pleas to stay put or not hearing them through the rush of blood through his ears. Adam shifted in his saddle, flicked his reins, and held his pistol in a wavering hand. After closing the distance to within forty yards, he shouted, "This good enough or should I get closer?"

Cale wore a wide-brimmed hat that was the same shade of black as the long, greasy hair that flowed past his shoulders. A mustache hung beneath his nose like a stringy collection of horse mane that had been glued to his upper lip. Even though Adam was close enough to hit him using the .44 and apparently more than willing to do so, Cale sat easily in his saddle with his pistol resting across one knee. "You got the money you owe us or not?" he asked.

"We've got money!" Mia said.

Without taking his eyes off Cale, Adam pointed his gun at the other man and said, "Shut up, Mia! We don't have enough."

"I'll take whatever you got," Cale replied in his easygoing manner. "And if it ain't enough, I'm sure me and your sister can work something out." The smile that slid onto his face caused both ends of his mustache to curve upward. The lurid expression was matched by both of the men on either side of him.

"The hell you will," Adam said. "You'll deal with me and no one else."

"Afraid it's a bit late for that. We warned you it would come to this, Weyland. Now it's time to pay the piper." With that, Cale brought up his pistol to aim at Adam. "If you don't got the money you owe . . . and I know you don't . . . maybe the deed to your property and this house will suffice."

When the next shot cracked through the air, Mia jumped and screamed her brother's name as if that was to be the last thing he would ever hear her say. But no smoke plumed from Cale's pistol. None came from the guns held by any of the other men or even her brother. Instead, Cale reeled back in his saddle and grabbed his head. While he wavered back and forth on the verge of toppling to the ground, the distinct ratcheting sound of a rifle lever being worked came from behind Mia's horse. The fourth man may have been standing with the sun to his back, but Mia could tell he had a rifle to his shoulder and was taking aim.

"What's the meaning of this?" the former statue asked.

Those words were enough for Mia to recognize the voice as Slocum's. She looked at him with renewed hope that she and Adam might live to see another sunrise.

When she saw Cale slip from his saddle and drop to the ground, Mia felt a touch of relief. Unfortunately, when the two other men that had been riding with Cale saw that, all hell broke loose.

5

Paul pulled his horse around while drawing his pistol to fire a few quick shots. Since he was more concerned with not trampling his fallen partner, he wasn't focusing on placing his shots well enough to hit their intended target. Adam responded to that by firing a shot of his own, sending his bullets through the air too hastily to draw any blood. The moment a shot blazed in from his right, he shifted his aim toward the rider that had circled around to flank him.

Slocum fired his rifle, levered in another round, and shouted, "Mia, get down!"

That warning finally cut through the panic that gripped her like a cold iron fist. She leaned down to press her face against her horse's neck and prayed for the storm to pass over her head.

Now that he had a clear line of fire, Slocum aimed carefully and squeezed his trigger. The Winchester bucked against his shoulder and sent its round toward the rider that had circled around the house to flank the Weylands. Hitting him at the same time he took his shot. The rider jerked back and yelped in pain or surprise before snapping his reins to get his horse moving. Since Slocum wasn't looking to put anyone into their grave just yet, he allowed the man to run away and shifted his attention to Paul.

Knowing exactly how many rounds were left in his Winchester, Slocum fired them at a steady pace. He aimed at both Adam and the other rider, doing his best to get close without hitting either one of them. As soon as his rifle ran dry, he dropped it back into the saddle boot, drew his Colt Navy, and rode over to where Mia was waiting.

"Are you all right?" he asked.

She was still hugging her horse's neck and wasn't about to let go. "I think so," she replied shakily. "How's Adam?"

"That's what I'm about to find out," Slocum said before snapping his reins to approach the two men closest to him.

Cale lay on the ground, writhing in pain and kicking his heels against the dirt while pressing both hands against his head. Blood seeped from between his fingers, which wasn't a surprise since even the smallest head wounds bled terribly. If Cale was still moving and squawking, Slocum figured the wound wasn't so bad at all.

"Who the hell are you?" Paul asked.

"Just a concerned bystander," Slocum said. "Looks to me like you were about to harm this man and his sister."

"Do you know what this asshole did to bring us here?"

Looking over to Adam, Slocum replied, "I think I have a good idea."

"Then you should also know he's into us for over five thousand dollars."

"Gambling debt?"

"Hell no! He rode with us on a string of robberies outside of Amarillo. The cowardly little shit didn't have the sand to kill a few stagecoach drivers and cost us the whole job."

"So you're guessing about that money?"

"He didn't just cause that job to go up in smoke," Cale said from his spot on the ground. "When he skinned out on us, he took most of the money we'd rounded up along the way. He was always going on about helping pay off his debts, a patch of land, and that there house."

Mia straightened up to glare at her brother even harder than any of the gunmen. "Is that true? Did the one decent contribution you made to this family come from blood money?"

Adam didn't have much of anything to say to that, so he just shrugged and kept his eyes focused on anything but his sister.

Finally flopping over so he could sit upright, Cale looked at Slocum. Before his chin even lifted halfway to where it needed to be, he was swaying like a thin weed in a stiff breeze. "Why isn't anyone shooting this son of a bitch?"

"Because," Slocum said while locking eyes with Paul, "he knows better."

"Do you know who I am? I'm Cale Terrigan! Nobody steals from me and gets away with it." Clenching his eyes shut after another attempt at looking up, he added, "And nobody steals from me without paying the price."

"How much are you owed?" Slocum asked.

"Five thousand and thirty-eight dollars."

"How much of that is interest?"

Finally, Cale had collected himself enough to open his eyes and point them at Slocum without getting too dizzy to stay upright. "That ain't no business of yours."

"Adam, how much money do you have in your house?"

"I don't know."

"I do," Mia said. "But there's not even a quarter of that inside."

"Well, get what you've got," Slocum said. "That's only fair. Right, Cale?"

Still rubbing his head, Cale struggled to pull himself to his feet. Even though he needed Slocum's help to stand, he jerked his arm away angrily the moment he was up. He placed a hand gingerly upon his head where his stringy hair was plastered down by a thick layer of blood. For the moment, the flow seemed to have stopped, but it still made an impressive mess on his hand. After scooping up his hat, he said, "You shot me, mister. I don't take kindly to that."

"Well, that's between you and me. Certainly not you and her."

"At least give me your name."

"John Slocum."

Cale nodded. "Go get my fucking money."

"Since she's the only one who knows where it is, I'll be accompanying her," Slocum said. "And if Adam happens to get shot, stabbed, punched, or otherwise harmed while I'm gone, I'll just assume you mean to pick a fight with me as well. Trust me when I tell you the shot to knock you off your horse was a lot harder than the one it would have taken to kill you."

"I hear you." Despite the fact that it obviously hurt like a bear, Cale put his hat back on. "Just don't count on that threat lasting for too long."

Slocum nodded and motioned for Mia to lead the way to her house. She did so and was quick about it. Apart from the collection of horses and riders that had done the shooting, the only other signs of life in the area were a few nervous faces peeking out from behind the curtains of the house on the far left. Either the people in the house where Cale had been waiting weren't home or they were too scared to step foot outside.

When Mia climbed down from her saddle and approached her door, Slocum leaned over and whispered, "Bring me half of what you've got stashed and slip me the other half."

"But they said—"

"No time to argue. Just do what I say."

She nodded and hurried inside.

Slocum turned his horse around so he could watch the front door from the corner of his eye while also keeping track of what Cale and his men were doing. The one who'd flanked Mia and Adam had not only returned, but circled back around to join his partners. At least, he tried to join them before Slocum shouted, "That's close enough!"

When the other man looked to Cale for instructions, all he got was a hasty nod and a dismissive wave. The flanker held his ground and pointed his gun at Adam.

True to her word, Mia emerged from the house in no time at all. She stopped and pretended to fuss with the front door as she whispered, "I've got it, but there's less than I thought. I forgot I had to pay for food and supplies last week."

"Just cut it in half and tuck one portion under my knee."

She already had the money sectioned into two pieces and leaned over as if to look past Slocum's horse at Cale and the others. Her right hand slipped behind Slocum's knee to tuck a small bundle of bills between it and the horse's side.

"Come on now," Cale hollered. "I won't hurt you. Least, not yet anyway."

As Mia climbed into her saddle, Slocum watched carefully for any sign that Cale or his men were going to step out of line. When she nervously flicked her reins to ride toward the group of men, he reached down to snatch the money that he'd been holding in place with his knee. Slocum stuck the money into a pocket under his jacket and covered the movement by flipping the jacket open to retrieve some fresh rounds from his gun belt.

"Hand it over," Cale demanded.

Slocum nodded to her and Mia rode just close enough to the gunman to flip a bundle of cash at him.

Cale caught it after the money bounced off his chest and spread the bills apart between his thumb and forefinger. "Ain't much here," he grunted.

"That's what I told you," she said.

"A long ways from what you promised, even."

"We had bills to pay. Food to buy. You can get the rest later."

"No. I think I'll take the rest out of your pretty little ass right now."

By the time Cale's men closed in around Mia and Adam, Slocum had reloaded his Colt. He snapped it shut and aimed from the hip while saying, "That's what you get now. You'll get the rest later. I won't tell you again."

"You," Cale said while stabbing a finger at Slocum. "Shut the fuck up. This bitch is comin' with us to pay what she owes."

The man who'd had the flanking position earlier was now close enough to lunge forward to try and grab Mia. Unfortunately for him, he was close enough to her brother to catch the full brunt of Adam's blow when he slammed the side of his pistol into his nose. The gunman howled in pain as he pressed a hand against his face to stanch the blood that had started to flow. While he was still reeling, his gun was taken away from him by the same man who'd just surprised him with the vicious blow.

After one barked command from Cale, Paul raised his pistol and glared at Slocum.

"Take the bitch!" Cale said.

Slocum only had time to warn him with a simple, "Don't."

But Paul's loyalty to Cale was stronger than his fear of Slocum because he twisted around to reach for her while taking aim with his gun. Slocum waited for the moment when Paul was distracted between his two tasks before taking quick aim and squeezing his trigger. The instant the Colt Navy sent its round through the air, Slocum could tell he was on the money.

Sure enough, Paul was spun around by the hot lead that ripped through the left portion of his chest. He fell over and hit the dirt like a sack full of bricks, dead before he rolled to a stop.

"Pick up his gun, Mia," Slocum said.

She was rattled, but did as she was told. When Cale fixed a murderous glare on her, she reflexively brought the gun up to point in his general direction. Her hands were shaking and fear was evident in her eyes, which gave Cale an extra dose of confidence when he said, "You'd best shoot me now, girl."

"I wouldn't ask her to do that," Slocum said while striding up to stand by her side. "Especially since I'd be more than happy to oblige."

"Then go ahead and do it because I'll just be coming after you later."

"You've got all the money you're gonna get," Slocum said. "You were going to get the rest, but since you decided to try kidnapping an innocent woman, consider the remainder of the debt paid by me allowing you to live."

Cale shifted his weight, which was enough to make Slocum tighten his grip on his Colt and point it directly at his face. Without being told, Cale dropped his gun.

"See?" Slocum mused. "Making better decisions already. Now get out of my sight before I change my mind about this one."

Nodding slowly, Cale slapped the surviving gunman on the shoulder and told him, "Get on your horse, Bryce. We're leaving."

Although Bryce tried to put on a hard exterior, it was difficult for him to be too threatening when tears were streaming from his eyes after being cracked in the nose with the side of a revolver. He stuck his foot into a stirrup, slipped out, placed his foot in it again, and hauled himself onto the waiting animal's back.

"This ain't over, Weyland," Cale said.

"Make sure that it is," Slocum was quick to say. "Because if there is a next time, you and anyone else you bring along will end up like that one on the ground there."

All eyes shifted to Paul, but the man with the broken

nose was having a hard time looking away when Cale told him, "Pick him up and take him with us. We'll put him in the ground proper since these murdering pricks will probably just let him lay there to rot."

"Damn right we would," Adam said. "That's what you do to a dead rodent. Let it do some good by feeding a few coyotes."

Cale continued to nod as if a sort of uneasy peace had descended upon him. "Keep talkin', Weyland. That's what got you in this mess to begin with."

"We'll leave you to it," Slocum said. "Just so you know, if I see you again, I'll shoot first and figure it's in self-defense."

"That's a wise policy," Cale said.

All of the riders climbed into their saddles and the dead one was tossed over the back of his horse, where it was led by the reins toward town. Slocum let Mia and Adam go ahead while he lagged behind to make sure Cale wasn't going to try and come at him again before leaving. Whether it was out of fatigue or good sense, the gunmen rode away and didn't look back.

After losing sight of them, Slocum snapped his reins and hurried to catch up with Adam and Mia.

"You think we'll see them again?" she asked.

"That depends," Slocum replied while looking over at Adam. "How'd you build up that much of a debt?"

"Some of it's from gambling. Most was just like he said." Suddenly losing the ability to look either of the other two in the eye, Adam said, "I ran with them for a while in Amarillo. To be honest, I never thought I'd live long enough to regret it. When Cale first came to Bickell, he said everything would be forgiven so long as I pay him back piece by piece and that's what I've been doing."

"With what?" Mia asked. "The only money I ever give you is to buy supplies or food." When her brother couldn't even dredge up the strength to nod, she whispered, "You spent that money on whiskey? Jesus, Lord in Heaven. What are you doing to this family?"

Adam stared at her as he growled, "Call me any name you want, but don't spout that church talk to me again!"

They rode back to the trail to Louisiana in silence. When they met up with Triedle, Slocum cut off the inevitable inquiries with, "Don't even ask how it went. Let's just make up for lost time."

6

If Slocum thought the ride away from the Weyland house was quiet, the rest of that day was a funeral march. They camped that night in a spot just off the trail beside a shallow watering hole. Adam dug a bottle of liquor from his saddlebag and fell asleep with it in his arms. Mia cooked up some of the bacon Slocum provided, but didn't say more than two words along the way. Triedle stopped making conversation when he realized he was only talking to himself and Slocum wasn't in the mood to try and turn the somber mood around.

The next day, they woke to a breakfast of sticky oatmeal and strong coffee, watered the horses, bundled up their things, and struck out to the east. Slocum pushed the entire group to ride as fast as their horses would carry them. They started off at a crisp pace, built to a steady gallop, and maintained it until the animals worked up a lather. Slocum called for a stop at a creek, gave the horses a rest, and got the group moving again before Adam had enough time to find his bottle or sulk to anyone who'd pay him any mind.

By the time they were ready to stop for the night, nobody in the group had enough wind in their sails to say more than a few words. Mia gathered up some odds and ends from all the saddlebags, which were just enough to make a strangely appetizing stew if she'd had some meat to go along with it. Triedle opted to strike out to see if he might be able to scare up some game and disappeared for a while. Adam went to his saddlebag and then wandered off in the opposite direction.

"Where's he going?" Slocum asked.

Mia shrugged and peeled one of the two potatoes that Triedle had contributed to their supper. "Probably off to drink on his own. He prefers it that way."

"Well, that's a shame," Slocum said in a voice that was loud enough to be heard by anyone in the vicinity. "Because we could sure use another man out hunting for some fresh meat."

"Then you can take yer rifle and go!" Adam shouted back.

Shaking her head, Mia said, "He never was very helpful."

Slocum sat down on the blanket he'd thrown across the back of a large, half-buried rock. "I know he's your brother and all, but why do you put up with him? Surely this can't be the first time he's gotten you into a tough spot."

"It isn't, but ever since he found out he's sick, each spot's seemed tougher than the last."

"Sick? How sick?"

"The doctors don't agree on what it is. Some say it's consumption. Others say it's some kind of fever he picked up when he went into Mexico and has never able to shake. Whatever it is, it's going to be with him until . . ." She winced as if she'd stuck her finger into the campfire and then continued to peel with added vigor. "It's going to be with him for a long time, but we can make do."

"Is that when he started drinking?"

"No, but it's when he started drinking as if he was in a

competition to see how many bottles he could drain. He says it helps take the edge off."

"I'll bet it does."

Her eyes locked on to his and her brow furrowed into an angry crease. "Are you saying he's not in any pain? You've never been there to see him cough up blood or double over because he can't bear to stand up straight."

"I'm saying he may be sick, but that's not why he's drinking the way he does."

"Like you know anything about it," she grumbled as she shifted her attention back to her chore.

Slocum considered letting the matter drop. After all, he wasn't a preacher whose job was to sympathize with everyone's problems and Adam wasn't his brother. Just as he was feeling good about his decision and enjoying the crackle of the fire, Mia set one potato down to swap it out with the other.

"Do you know anything about it?" she asked.

As much as Slocum wanted to keep his mouth shut, he didn't want to ignore Mia's timid question or insult her by getting up and walking away. "There are plenty of sick men in the world," he told her. "Some try to push on with their lives and others get lost in feeling sorry for themselves."

"Sometimes there's a lot for one man to feel sorry about."

Slocum raised an eyebrow and looked at her silently. It seemed that was enough to break down whatever wall she'd built up between herself and him since she'd started peeling.

"I know," she said. "He's been sick for over a year. I don't expect him to skip across town every day and click his heels when he rounds a corner, but I didn't expect him to get this bad either. I just figured he was going through a hard time and needed to get over it at his own pace."

"That's just what he's doing."

"Really?"

"Yeah," Slocum replied without encouraging the optimism in her voice. "He's getting over it by drowning his problems in whiskey and trying to get himself killed before the sickness gets to him."

"Oh my God," she said.

Slocum didn't like seeing the dismay on her face or hearing the despair in her voice. He hated even more knowing that he was the one to put those things there. "You must have known that already. I mean, you're forced to deal with him every day."

"Yes, but I don't want to think about my brother dying."

"Haven't you thought about it ever since you heard the news from them doctors? I've only known Adam for a short time, but I doubt he'd be the sort to keep that much of a secret."

She looked in the direction her brother had gone and couldn't find him. Even so, she lowered her voice when she said, "He cried like a baby for weeks. I've never pitied anyone worse. And don't you say a word to him about that. The only reason I mentioned it was so you know he wasn't always like the man you've seen."

"I figured as much. You know how? Because I've seen plenty of men like him. Hell, I've been a man like him at one time or another."

"You've been sick?" she asked.

Slocum shook his head. "That's not what I mean. I've tried drowning a part of myself so I don't have to look at it no more. I've also found the prospect of dying appealing enough to seek it out every now and then."

As she shook her head, Mia peeled the potato at the same quickening pace. "He's not that way."

"Is that why he became an outlaw in Amarillo?"

She shook her head. "That was a rough patch, is all. When he parted with the family for that time, we all thought he was going to seek more doctors. I barely heard a word from him, even when we lost all of our family but me. I think he did what he did in Amarillo because he was a lost soul."

"Really? Is that what you see?"

Although she wasn't about to say as much, the fleeting look she shot at him was loaded with enough expression to tell Slocum he'd hit a nerve.

"You may not like hearing it, but you know there's more to it than that," he said. "He's either convinced bullets will bounce off of his chest or he's looking to catch one straight through his heart. Whatever sickness he's got doesn't matter anymore. Not so long as he's infected with the idea that it's better to be dead than alive."

"When did you ever feel that way, John? How could you know so much?"

"I've lost good friends. Seen loved ones killed in front of me. I've also filled more graves than I can count. Even if there was a good reason to pull the trigger every single one of them times, it still haunts a man no matter how hard you may be." Slocum stared into the flames, narrowing his eyes as if his will alone was enough to make them flare up or die down. "There's something that creeps into a man's eyes when those ghosts are nipping at his heels. It makes him wonder if he wouldn't be better off anywhere but in this world. Sometimes it makes him sloppy and reckless. Other times, he knows exactly what he's doing. There's nothing sloppy about it. That's the look that's in your brother's eyes, Mia. You know the one I mean."

It took her a few moments and a whole lot of effort, but she eventually nodded. "I do know. The doctors say his sickness may make him unsteady sometimes. In the head, I mean. But I've known Adam all my life and he's not crazy. I'd know if that happened because that's what happened to our mother. She lost her mind slowly. You could see it as if the person I knew was leaking out from a jar. Adam has his moments, but he's not that far along yet."

"What made your mother that way?"

"The doctors didn't know for certain," she said. "They tried plenty of things to help her and wanted to try plenty more. We moved to a more temperate climate to try and help ease her mind, but when that didn't work, the doctors wanted to put her through treatments that were just . . . cruel. I was a little girl at the time and I thought those men wanted to torture her because she was wicked. My father wouldn't stand for it. He said he'd rather see her shrivel up in her own bed than hand her over to barbarians." Although she smirked at that, there was no humor in her expression. "In those years, we never went to a doctor again. Not even when Adam busted his leg. My father swore they were all just men who used fancy words to cover up the fact that they didn't know anything. After my mother died, it was hard to disagree with that."

She finished with her peeling and reached for a dented pot that Slocum had been using to cook everything from chicory coffee to possum stew. Placing the pot between her feet, she used the knife in her hands to start cutting the potatoes into large chunks, which landed in the pot with dull clanging tones. "You don't know how hard it was to get Adam to go to a doctor when his condition started up," she said. "He said it was the same thing our mother had and that there wasn't any hope. I told him it was different and maybe another doctor might know something more."

"Do you think it's the same thing?"

"Could be, I suppose. Seems worse, though. Then again, it may be that our father kept her in her room and away from us children when she was going through the worst of it. None of that matters, though. The doctors still don't know much of anything and I've got to deal with Adam whether I know what's wrong with him or not." She started to say something else, but stopped when she heard approaching footsteps. Both she and Slocum turned toward them and waited.

Stepping around a cluster of large rocks, Triedle smiled proudly and extended his arm to show them a small rabbit dangling from his fist. "Told you I wouldn't come back empty-handed!"

"Damn close to it," Slocum chuckled. "That rabbit's mostly skin and bones. Maybe you should tie it to a hook and use it for bait to catch something bigger."

"Eh, to hell with you," Triedle said as he walked toward the campfire.

"Why don't you skin that squab over there?" Slocum said. "We may have to pick stringy meat from our teeth, but at least it's something."

"To hell with you a second time! I went out and got this thing. You can clean it up."

"Give it to Adam," Mia said. "He's always been good at preparing game."

"Yeah," Slocum said while working a kink from his neck. "Give it to Adam. Nobody's getting a free ride."

Triedle scowled down at him and asked, "What about you? Seems like you're content to do a fat load of nothing."

"I'm leading this trail drive, which means the rest of you get to pull your weight when we're not actually driving."

When Triedle looked at her for support, Mia said, "John saved my life once already. I don't mind cooking up some stew."

Knowing he wasn't going to get much more than that from anyone in sight, he looked around and asked, "Where is that wild man anyway?"

"Headed off in that direction. Shouldn't be far."

Triedle grumbled under his breath and walked in the direction Slocum was pointing. The only way he could have protested any louder would be for him to stomp his feet and wail.

"Do you think he's going to be a problem?" Mia asked.

"Nothing I can't handle," Slocum said. "He may grouse a lot, but he does know his way around a poker game."

"Not him. Adam. After what happened back at our house, I wouldn't blame you if you wanted to be rid of us for good."

"How much cash did you take from there?"

"You didn't count it before you gave it back to me?" she asked.

"Not mine to count."

Mia nodded and smiled warmly, stowing that bit of information away. "Just over three hundred dollars. We used to own the house next door to us. The one where those men were waiting. They might have even thought they were at the house where we live, since we don't bother telling everyone in Bickell about our business. Anyway, we sold it and that's where the money came from. Adam's pissed away most of it." Mia's face twitched and she looked about as if expecting someone to step from the shadows to discipline her for her language.

"That should be enough to help us along the way," Slocum said. "And once we get to Louisiana, I should be able to scare up enough to get you on your feet. It's a start a least. I'm sorry I couldn't get it all for you."

She shook her head vigorously. "No, you were right to do what you did. Adam's the one who owes Cale. Considering we bought the house with what he stole from those men, the money we made from selling it isn't really ours, and I'm not sorry to see it go. If anything," Mia added while looking up to focus her gaze on something over Slocum's shoulder, "he should be sorry for putting us in that predicament."

Slocum barely had to glance back there to know that Adam was standing at the edge of the glow given off by the fire.

No matter what passed between brother and sister in that moment, it was lost on the gambler, who walked straight up to Adam and slapped the scrawny dead rabbit against his chest.

"Here," Triedle said. "Clean this while I wash up in that sorry excuse for a stream over there."

Adam took the rabbit, walked over to his saddlebag to get his hunting knife, and spat a wad of bloody juice onto the ground between Slocum and Mia.

"It's gonna be a long ride to Louisiana," Slocum grumbled.

7

They probably could have made it to Dallas if Slocum had pushed them hard enough. If anyone complained too much, he would have been more than happy to cut them loose so they could fend for themselves without him having to hear any more complaints. As it was, Adam spent his time quietly sulking and Mia spent hers looking after him. Triedle must have sensed he was drifting too close to Slocum's bad side because he did whatever was needed of him without pressing too hard about what they would do once they reached New Orleans. The Louisiana border was still a ways off and he was content to scout ahead or chase after the occasional bit of wild game flushed from nearby bushes alongside the trail.

And somehow, despite having those three with him, Slocum couldn't help feeling a heavier solitude than if he'd been riding that trail alone. Talk was sparse in camp and the conversations were uncomfortable simply because everyone was walking on eggshells to keep from setting someone off.

With Slocum and Adam being so near to the end of their ropes, that made for a whole lot of eggshells.

When he spotted a small town in the distance, Slocum nearly stood up in his stirrups without reining his horse to a stop. "Look there!" he shouted.

Nobody responded since they didn't seem to hear him over the rumble of the horses galloping over the dried terrain. Slocum pulled back on his reins and motioned for everyone to do the same. Once the other three were settling in around him, Slocum pointed to the buildings clustered together in the distance and asked, "Anyone know what town that is?"

"Is that Dallas?" Mia asked.

"We've been covering plenty of ground," Triedle said, "but not enough to make it to Dallas quite yet."

"I say we stop there for the night," Adam said.

Mia cast a stern look at him and grumbled, "You just want to get to a saloon."

Slocum removed his hat and wiped the sweat from his brow using the back of his forearm. "If that's true, then for once me and him are in agreement. And before you stare a hole through me, Mia, I say there ain't no way to keep your brother away from whiskey. There's plenty of it out in the world and right now I want some for myself."

"Amen to that!" Triedle proclaimed.

"Then it's unanimous," Slocum said while placing his hat back upon his head. "Whatever town that is, we're headed there."

"Excuse me!" Mia said. "I didn't agree to that."

"You're right." Just when she started to smile at that, Slocum added, "It's not unanimous. It's just decided."

Adam let out something that seemed like a laugh. At least it was the closest he'd gotten to one in recent memory. "A warm bed instead of cold dirt under me for a change. That should be nice."

"I suppose so," she said grudgingly. "We haven't touched any of our traveling money yet, so a few hotel rooms shouldn't do any harm."

"Don't go digging into your life savings just yet, my good woman," Triedle said. "I propose John and I put our partnership to the test for the greater good." Holding out a hand to Slocum to stop him before he could protest, Triedle added, "We strike up a game in yonder saloon and whatever winnings we collect go toward any expenses incurred while in town. How much money do you have in your pockets, Adam?"

"Maybe two dollars."

"Then that's all you get unless your sister decides to add any more to it."

One stern shake of her head was all Adam needed to see before he went back to sulking.

"On the other hand," Triedle continued, "if he decides to join us for a game and we win, then the fair thing to do is for him to keep his winnings."

"Great," Mia said. "Once again, he drinks his money away while the rest of us have to pay for little things like room and board."

"A percentage, then."

When Slocum said those words, all three of the others shifted to look at him. It was a much more pleasant surprise for Triedle and Adam than it was for Mia.

"He can keep a percentage," Slocum explained. "Just like anyone else who's paying his way in this world."

"Fine," Mia said spitefully. "Since nobody gives a damn about what I say, then I'll just stop saying anything."

Triedle knew better than to push her, so he set his sights on the town and started thinking about his poker strategies.

Adam rolled his eyes, leaving Slocum as the only one to hold her gaze.

"It's decided, then."

* * *

The town's name was Darnell, which also happened to be the name of the largest hotel, two restaurants, and the loudest saloon. As anxious as he was to get something in his belly other than water and potatoes, Slocum's first order of business was to find a suitable place to put up the horses. After all the miles they'd covered so far, the least he could do was see to it they got a night in a good stable while everyone else indulged themselves. He wasn't surprised in the least that the first place he found was Darnell Livery.

"Look at him," Slocum said as he, Mia, and Triedle walked down the street through the middle of town. "He's happier than he's been since I met him."

Nodding as she watched Adam hurry ahead of them, she said, "Yes, he's practically skipping . . . right to that saloon. Lovely. What do you care whether he's happy or not? Mostly, you just like it when he's not bothering you."

"Exactly. Once he gets some time to himself in a saloon, maybe some companionship for the night along with a bottle, he won't be bothering me for a while."

"You mean after the card game, right?" Triedle asked.

"Yes, Ed. After the card game."

"You seem to have changed your mind about a few things over the last few days," Mia pointed out. "Just yesterday you threatened to tie Ed to the back of your horse and drag him for two miles if he mentioned poker again."

Slocum shrugged and tucked his hands into his pockets so his steps could become more of a stroll. "Sometimes a man needs to realize when he's being carried on a current instead of steering the boat. Things go a lot easier when you take the time to enjoy drifting every now and then."

Rolling her eyes and shaking her head, Mia asked, "How much do you need to get nailed into your game?"

"Nailed into my game?"

"She means staked," Triedle said. "Staking us for the game. Is that right?"

"Does that mean giving you enough money to start playing?" she asked.

"Yes, ma'am, it does."

"Then that's what I mean." She dug into her dress pocket to retrieve the bundle of money. Peeling off several bills, she handed them to Slocum and asked, "Is this enough?"

"Not really," he told her. "Just keep it."

She peeled off some more, which amounted to roughly half of it and handed that over. "What about this?"

Triedle's mouth was practically watering as he eyed the money. When he caught sight of the saloon and looked back at the cash, be was chomping at the bit.

"We've got enough to start a game," Slocum said. "And if this goes the way it should, we won't need any more."

"But having more at the start will speed things along, won't it?" she asked.

"Yes, ma'am, it will," Triedle said anxiously.

Slocum shot him a stern look, which meant he didn't see Mia's hand moving toward him until it had already stuffed the money into his shirt pocket.

"Take this, get your game going, and do whatever it is you're looking to do," she ordered. "And before you protest on the assumption that I'm trying to be generous, you should know I'm expecting my percentage. Is that the proper term, John? Percentage?"

"Yes, Mia," he replied, feeling the bite of her sarcasm as though it were a set of teeth nipping at his ear.

"Then I'll want my percentage of your winnings."

There was a good amount of fatigue and aggravation written into her features. He recognized that well enough because he'd been feeling plenty of it himself over the last few days. But beneath that, there was a glint of hope shining like a jewel that had been buried at the bottom of a river and uncovered only after the roughest waters had flowed over it.

"And," she said resolutely, "this should mean your game

will get results sooner rather than later, just as you promised."

"I didn't promise anything," Slocum pointed out.

Triedle was quick to jump in with, "Yeah. We can't promise anything where poker's concerned."

Mia's jaw was set in a firm line as she nodded once. "All right. I can promise you one thing, though. If we're not back on the trail by noon tomorrow, there'll be hell to pay." She then veered away from the two men, stomped across a path of boards that had been pressed into the ground on either side of the street, and pulled open the door to the Darnell Steak House so she could go inside.

A fat drop of water splattered on the brim of Slocum's hat, followed by another one that slapped against his cheek just beneath his eye when he looked up at a sky that was now covered with clouds. In the space of a few seconds, more and more drops hit nearby rooftops or landed in the street.

"If I didn't know any better," Triedle said while pulling up the collar of his jacket to keep the rain from trickling down his back, "I'd say you just got replaced as the leader of this gang."

"You think so?" Slocum asked as he held out the money he'd fished from his pocket and showed it to him. "So long as I'm the gang's treasurer, you'd better stay on my good side."

"I don't know about that either. Since she was the one to hand out the money, I'd say . . ."

"What?" Slocum growled. "What do you want to say?"

Triedle put on a smile that only widened as the rain began to pour down on him and Slocum. "I'd say it's time we got inside and played some poker!"

8

Slocum still had rainwater in his clothes by the time he, Adam, and Triedle had doubled their money. The Darnell Saloon was a small place with a bar consisting of a few crates stacked end to end, three round tables, and a fireplace that took up most of one wall. Of the four hours they'd been there, one hour had been spent pulling together another two people willing to play for money and a good portion of the next had been pissed away in getting Adam to simmer down and stop trying to pick a fight with a fellow strumming a banjo in the corner closest to the door. After that was cleared up, Slocum had yet to find a spot to place his chair where it wasn't dripping on him from the sieve that passed for a roof.

"What've you got, mister?" asked a tall man with dark eyes who'd been the first to sit down when Triedle had started shuffling the cards.

Slocum laid down his two pair, just in time for the top card to get hit by a falling drop of water. "Eights and nines," he announced.

"Don't beat my three sixes!"

59

"Nope," Triedle said from the other side of the table, "but these five hearts sure do!"

When he tried to scoop up the pot, Triedle's arm was grabbed by the man with the sixes. The fourth fellow at the table, a grizzled rancher with a beard that somehow covered more than half his face, raised an eyebrow and watched the proceedings as if they were a stage show.

"You two are in on it together," the man with the sixes said. "You're partners and you're cheats."

"There's nothing wrong with playing cards with a friend," Triedle said.

"There is if you're running some kinda dodge."

"What proof have you got that we're cheating, other than you're losing?"

"I don't need proof."

"The hell you don't," Slocum growled. When the others looked at him, he drew a hunting knife from the scabbard hanging from his belt and stuck it into the table. "You want to make accusations? Then back them up. You can even take that knife if it'll make you any braver. If you don't have any proof, then I suggest you shut your goddamn pie-hole."

"Yeah," the rancher said. "Shut yer pie-hole."

Triedle's eyebrows waggled as he said, "You want to accuse someone of cheating? Why don't you start with that one there? He's the big winner of this game."

Nobody could deny that statement. Although Slocum and Triedle's combined winnings placed them ahead in the game, it wasn't nearly as big a margin as the rancher was enjoying. Finally, the man with the sixes had to give up his hand, his argument, as well as his contribution to the pot. As the game got rolling again, the natural ebb and flow turned in his favor and that was the end of his accusations of cheating.

Once Triedle had stopped whining about getting into a game and Adam had gone to the bar to spend his percentage,

Slocum actually began to enjoy himself. When he returned from taking a stroll to get something to eat, he found two locals had sat down to fill his spot. Even more sat down to play once Triedle walked away for a while. Judging by the talk that circulated the saloon in his absence, everyone had picked up on the fact that he was a professional card player. Some of the other players took that as a warning, while others accepted it as a challenge to see if they could unseat someone who made his living playing the odds. No matter what complaints or taunts went back and forth regarding the newcomers in town, the players were anxious for his return and the game flourished.

The game continued for another hour, which was enough time for Slocum's drinks to make their rounds through his system. He excused himself from the table, paid a visit to the outhouse, and returned just as the table erupted in laughter from one of Triedle's off-color jokes. Slocum had his eyes focused on the back of his chair, which meant they were at just the right level to catch an impressive pair of breasts displayed by a woman in a dark green dress with a plunging neckline.

"Hello there," she said while stepping directly between Slocum and the card table. "My name's Natasha."

He took a moment to drink in the sight of her. Natasha was only slightly taller than average for a woman, but her other attributes were well above that standard. The pale, creamy skin of her chest was accentuated nicely by the color and cut of her dress as well as by the long, dark red hair that flowed over both shoulders. She smiled at him with full, juicy lips to show just a bit more gum than teeth when they parted. Without hesitation, she placed her hands upon his chest and stepped up close enough to him that she could be heard when she whispered in a voice that was almost as smoky as the air in the saloon.

"You've been having a run of good luck," she said.

"Yes indeed," Slocum replied, placing his hand upon a firm, nicely rounded hip. "Something tells me it's about to get better."

Natasha's smile widened. "A man who goes after what he likes. That's a nice change from the drunks who normally come here. More often than not, I've got to lead them by the nose just to get them to touch me properly." Placing her hand over his and shifting her hips, she added, "And that is most definitely the proper way."

"Do you work here?"

"Yes, but I'm no whore if that's what you're thinking."

There were several jobs for women in saloons. When they were dressed the way Natasha was, that list shrank a bit. If she wasn't a whore, she was either a dancer or a saloon girl. There was no stage in sight, which narrowed the list down even further. Saloon girls were paid to keep customers happy and buying liquor. If they were truly good at their jobs, they could get the more expensive bottles off the top shelves before they ever had a chance to collect dust.

"Your friend sent me over to put a smile on your face," she said.

"Did he now? Then maybe you'd like to sit on my lap for a spell while I play the next few hands."

Pressing against him even more, she said, "Actually, I'm supposed to put that smile on your face right now and keep it there for a while. You know what I mean?"

Slocum leaned over to get a look at the table. He'd expected Triedle to send his regards with a wave or nod, but the gambler seemed just as surprised as Slocum by Natasha's presence. Shifting his gaze a few seats away from Triedle, Slocum finally got the acknowledgment he'd been after. It came from the rancher, whose luck had taken a turn for the worse before Slocum got up to relieve himself. The man tipped his hat and made a subtle motion with his hand as if he were politely shooing away a horsefly.

"*He* sent you?" Slocum asked.

Natasha ran her fingers along his collar and gently brushed her ample bosom against him. "That's right. He says you've been playing a long time and that you should take a little time to play with me."

That made sense. For the first half of the night, the rancher had been content to rake in his winnings and laugh at Triedle's jokes. Once luck began to smile on Slocum instead of him, the rancher got sick of losing and decided to do something about it. Since Slocum had been enjoying a few good hands in a row, he must have been pegged as the biggest competition at the table. The truth of the matter was that Slocum had known to call an obvious bluff and the rest had been sheer, dumb luck. If that was threatening enough to convince a rich rancher to do this for him just to get him out of the game for a while, then so be it. Slocum was enjoying the game, but some games were a hell of a lot better than others. There was still one thing that didn't quite line up, however.

"I thought you said you weren't a whore," he said as Natasha's hand slid down along his chest toward his belt.

"I'm not, but the fella who paid me doesn't know that. Instead of correcting him, I took his money and agreed to keep you busy for a while. As for the rest," she added while rubbing the erection that grew between Slocum's legs, "there's no reason we can't have our fun. I've been watching you since you put Smithee in his place."

"Who's Smithee?"

"The one that accused you and that gambler of cheating a while back. He's been trying to get under my skirts for weeks, and right now I bet steam is just about to come out of his ears."

Slocum wrapped an arm around her and leaned in as if to kiss her ear. Instead, he brushed aside Natasha's hair and took a look at the table. Sure enough, Smithee was watching them intently. "I think you're right about that steam," he whispered. "If he's been annoying you, I wouldn't mind putting him in his place again."

"Just do me a favor and clean him out when we get back."

"If he's still here," Slocum said as he moved his hand down to cup her plump backside. "I intend on taking my time with you."

Her lips were close enough to his neck that he could feel them curl into a grin as she said, "He'll still be here. I can't afford to be away for too long, but I know you'll make it worth my time. I rent a room across the street. Care to have a look?"

Whore or not, she was warm, willing, and knew exactly what to do to get Slocum's wheels turning. "Don't mind if I do," he said.

Natasha waved toward the bar, where two other ladies were waiting. One of them, a blonde with a slender build and long legs, strutted up to the table, placed her hand upon Smithee's shoulder, and took a seat on his lap. As long as she was able to keep the smile on his face that showed up then, there was no danger of him leaving that spot.

"Come along now," Natasha said while taking Slocum's hand and leading him to the front door. "I'm sure there'll be plenty more to win when you get back."

They crossed the street to a narrow building that was two windows wide and three floors tall. A sign marked the place as the Second Street Boardinghouse. Every step of the way, she teased him by rubbing against him in some way or another, leaning over to lick his neck or even tug at his clothes. Even though it was a short walk to the boardinghouse, it felt like a very long trip. After leading him up one flight of stairs, Natasha dug into a small pocket for a key that unlocked the last room at the end of a short hall.

"Here we are," she said while leading him inside. "Since I was just supposed to get you out of that saloon for a while, I suppose we could just sit and socialize for a spell."

Slocum grabbed her by the hips, slammed the door shut, and pushed her against it. The room was a little bigger than he'd expected and lit only by what light made it through the windows past a set of thick yellow curtains. Rather than say anything, he let his hands do his talking for him. They gathered up her skirts, pulled them up far enough for him to reach beneath them, and began exploring the smooth contours of her hips and upper thighs.

Natasha leaned her head against the door and slid one knee up along his leg. "I like that," she purred. When his hand made it beneath her undergarments to find the thatch of hair between her legs, she said, "And I like that even more! Perhaps we should move this to . . ."

Grinning while rubbing a slow circle around her swollen clit, Slocum asked, "Move this to where?" When she tried to speak again, he took her breath away a second time by rubbing his finger down to slide it in between the moist lips of her pussy.

"Nowhere," she finally sighed. "You just stay right where you are."

Natasha opened her legs and leaned most of her weight against the door. That way, his fingers could move in and out of her freely. Slocum kept that up for a few more seconds before easing his finger out of her. He kept his hand between her legs so he could rub the skin of her inner thighs.

Eventually, she lowered her leg and opened her eyes. "Think I should return the favor?"

"I suppose that would be civil," he replied. "Especially since I'm a guest in your room and all."

She smirked while pushing him back a few steps. Before he could move any farther, she was tugging at his belt and pulling his jeans down. Natasha lowered herself to both knees, grabbed his rigid cock, and wrapped her mouth around it. Her lips were soft and damp as they slid up and down along his shaft. Before long, Slocum was the one leaning against the door.

He let out a long breath and savored the feel of her mouth on his hard pole. Not only was she eager to make him feel good, but she knew what she was doing. As her lips moved down, they tightened around him, and when they slid up toward his tip, she teased him with her tongue. His pleasure quickly turned into impatience, and when he guided her to her feet, Natasha looked at him with wide-eyed anticipation.

"Didn't you like that?" she asked as if she didn't know the answer to that all too well.

Slocum pinned her against the door again, hiked her skirts all the way up to her waist, and said, "Sure, but I think we'll both like this a whole lot more."

She reached down to guide him between her legs. The moment he felt the tip of his erection touch her lips, he pushed forward to plunge it into her. Natasha let out a slow moan and wrapped her arms tightly around Slocum's shoulders. By the time he started pumping in and out of her, she'd lifted one leg to wrap it around his waist.

"Oh, God," she said. "That's just what I've been wanting all damn night. Fuck me harder."

Despite everything else that had happened and her forwardness so far, Slocum was surprised to hear her talk that way. It wasn't so much the words themselves that caught his attention, but the fierceness she put behind them. The primal tone in her voice and the way she ground her hips against him made Slocum even harder and his thrusts all the more urgent.

She gritted her teeth, pushed her head back, and pumped her hips in time to his rhythm. "Harder!"

Never one to disappoint a lady, Slocum reached down to cup her backside in both hands. Once he had a firm grip, he pulled her close and drove his cock into her with enough force to rattle the door on its hinges. Natasha showed her appreciation with a beaming smile and a loud moan. She even reached around to grab his hips and pull him toward her to make sure he never lost his momentum.

Suddenly, the door began to rattle with something that wasn't caused by her back slamming against it.

"Keep it down in there," a muffled voice said from the hall. "There's folks trying to sleep."

Both Slocum and Natasha froze.

She grinned at him like a girl who'd been caught rolling with a boy in the loft of her father's barn. He smirked as well and started massaging her buttocks. Slowly, he began grinding his hips until he was all the way inside her again.

"Move," she whispered. "I don't want any trouble. I live here, you know."

"You want me to move?" he asked. "How's this?"

She tried to push him back, but was distracted by the way his erect member shifted inside her. When he found just the right spot, she leaned back and knocked her head against the door.

"I mean it!" the grouchy neighbor squawked from what sounded like a few steps down the hall.

"Here," Slocum said as he stepped back and allowed her to regain her footing. "Wouldn't want you to get in any trouble."

She tugged at her clothes, but was much more concerned with scurrying past him to the other side of the room, where there was a modest, four-post bed covered by a multicolored quilt. As she fussed with the quilt, Slocum came up behind her and hiked her skirts up once again. "Just give me a moment," she said.

As soon as he got his hands on her bare hips again, he was stiffer than before and aching to pick up where they'd left off. "Don't have a moment to spare. I want you right now."

If she had anything to say against that, she kept it to herself while forgetting whatever she'd been doing with the quilt so she could just hang on to it with both hands. Natasha arched her back and tossed her red mane over her shoulders as she felt Slocum pound into her from behind.

As he ran his hands along the rounded slopes of her ass and pumped into her again and again, Slocum said, "Do something for me."

"Anything. Anything!"

"Remind me to buy that rancher fella a drink."

9

Adam stood at the bar, leaning upon his elbows as if his back wasn't strong enough to hold him up. His head hung low and his eyelids drooped. The only muscles that seemed to be working were the ones in the hand that was wrapped tightly around his whiskey glass. Those fingers cinched in a little tighter so he could lift the glass and slam it back down again.

"Gimme another!" he said.

The barkeep walked over to him with bottle in hand. "You got enough to pay for another?"

"What the hell difference does that make?"

"Plenty, since this is a business I'm running and not a charity for vagabonds."

"Vagabonds?" Adam snarled as he did his best to pull himself upright. "I'll have you know I'm with the men at that poker game! Without them, you wouldn't have all the business you're enjoying right now."

The barkeep looked over Adam's shoulder and then back to him. "What poker game?"

"The one that . . ." As he turned around to get a look at

Slocum and Triedle's table, Adam could only see empty chairs and a few restless locals nursing their drinks farther down the bar. "Oh, yeah," he said with a sloppy grin. "That was in the other place. Well, I left that behind because it was too loud and decided to come here. You should be thankful for any customers you can get!"

"I would be if they paid for their drinks."

"I did pay."

"Which brings me back to my first question," the barkeep said with the patience a man can get only after years of dealing with babbling brooks like Adam Weyland. "Do you have enough to pay for another?"

"Of course I do. Just pour."

Rather than take the glass from Adam's white-knuckled grip, he reached beneath the bar for another and filled it.

Without missing a beat, Adam took the glass, tossed the liquor down his throat, and slammed it next to the first one.

"Time to pay up, mister."

"You're right," Adam said with a slow nod and growing smile. "I am a vagabond and I don't have enough to pay for this drink." Swiping an arm across the top of the bar, he shattered the glasses against a wall and added, "Or those glasses."

"Son of a bitch!"

Adam was grinning from ear to ear as the barkeep reached across to grab the front of his shirt. When he spotted the ax handle the barkeep had picked up from wherever it had been stashed, he started to laugh.

"Oh, you think this is funny?" the barkeep asked.

"Most definitely."

"How about this?"

The barkeep's free hand snapped forward to knock the ax handle against the side of Adam's head. It wasn't a powerful blow, but was enough to take the wind from Adam's sails. His knees buckled, his hands slapped flat against the bar, and when the barkeep let go of him, he dropped straight to the floor.

As the barkeep stomped around the bar, he asked, "What about now? Still think it's funny?"

Adam started to say something, but his throat was quickly filled with vomit, which he spewed onto the tarnished foot rail he gripped with both hands for support.

Grabbing him by the back of his collar, the barkeep lifted Adam to his feet as if he were picking up a dog by the scruff of its neck. "Let's see what you've got on you," he said while using the ax handle to pin Adam against the front of the bar.

The moment he felt the barkeep's hands sifting through his pockets, Adam lashed out with his knee as well as both hands. If so much of his strength hadn't been sapped by the whiskey and the disease that coursed through his veins, he might have made a dent in the barkeep. As it was, he put on more of a show than a fight.

"Adam!" Mia shouted as she raced through the saloon's front door. "What are you doing?"

"This man's robbing me!"

"What?" the barkeep and Mia shouted simultaneously. Of the two, the barkeep looked more surprised. He overcame that by swinging her brother into the bar while Adam played it up by hitting the warped wood without even trying to cover his face or head. The impact was solid and accompanied by a crunch that could have been made by the breaking of planks or bone.

Mia rushed forward to grab the barkeep's arm before he could deliver a straight punch to her brother's face. "Stop it!" she shouted. "Let him go!"

Although the barkeep didn't try to break free or take his swing, he did look around at the few other customers in his place. "I wasn't robbing anyone! Someone tell this crazy woman that!"

One of the customers was an old man who looked dead on his feet. The other had the dirty face and crazy eyes of someone who'd wandered in from a storm after being raised by wolves. Apparently, neither of them had a good thing to say on the barkeep's behalf.

"Crazy woman?" Adam grunted. "You can't talk to her like that. My sister may be a tireless shrew, but she ain't crazy!" He followed that up by grabbing the barkeep's leg and sinking his teeth into his shin.

In his haste to pull away from Adam and any other restraint, the barkeep hopped back while trying to shake his leg free. Because Mia still had a hold of him, she was knocked off balance and shoved into a small table.

"What? You're who? Shit, I didn't mean to—"

But it was too late for explanations—not that Adam would have listened to them anyway. He sank his teeth in deeper when he bit the barkeep again, wrapping both arms around his leg as if he were afraid of being kicked into next week. Judging by the panicked look on the barkeep's face and the power that he put into his efforts to break loose, that wasn't exactly an unwarranted fear.

The ax handle dropped down onto Adam's shoulder and then thumped against his back. "You're both crazy!" he said while hitting Adam on the arm.

Mia tried to get up, but slipped as the table beneath her finally gave way. A pair of hands came to her aid, but drifted directly to her chest and stayed there. "That's good enough," she said as she regained her footing and turned to face the man who'd helped her back up. Seeing the lecherous smile on the old man's face, she immediately began swatting at him. "Get your hands off!"

Even as she slapped his face, the old man wouldn't stop smiling. A sharp kick to the groin gave her enough room to get away from his clumsy advances. When she approached the bar again, she found her brother still lying on the floor with the barkeep looming over him. "Get away from him!"

"You don't understand, lady!" the barkeep shouted. "He owes me for a drink."

"All this for a drink?" she asked.

"Don't believe him!" Adam said. "He's a robber!"

"And," the barkeep grunted while dusting himself off, "for the glasses he broke."

Having recovered from the jolt to his nether region, the old man waddled over to Mia and grabbed her ass with both hands. She yelped in surprise, turned around, and smacked him across the face. That lit an angry fire in the old man's eyes, which was quickly extinguished by the ax handle, which cracked against his ear.

Mia drew a sharp breath, followed the old man's descent to the floor, and then looked up at the ax handle, which still hung in the air a few feet away from her face. Tracing the length of chipped wood down to the hand that gripped it, she soon found herself looking at the barkeep's sweaty face.

"Drinks, glasses, and," the barkeep added between tired breaths, "for being an asshole. That's what this is about."

She nodded slowly and gazed down at Adam, who looked ready to vomit another mess onto the floor. "I suppose that does sound like my brother," she said.

"I don't care if it sounds like your mother or yer Aunt Tilly!" the barkeep roared. "I'll kill this son of a bitch if he don't pay up! Now get my money and get him the hell off of me!"

She stepped up to the bar, reached down to grab Adam's ear, and pulled. He stumbled back to his feet, only to knock his head against the bar as his legs flopped in every direction other than what was needed to get him up.

"You're taking his word over mine?" he asked.

She didn't stop pulling his ear until he was looking directly into her eyes. That's when she said, "It's probably worth more."

Using the back of his hand to wipe the drool and dirt from his mouth, Adam said, "Maybe it is."

"Do you have the money to pay this man?"

"Maybe."

"Look for it right now and be quick about it," she warned, "or I'll walk outside and let him resume looking for it himself."

Adam locked eyes with the barkeep as he reached into his pockets one at a time. He checked his pants pockets, shirt pocket, and finally the watch pocket in his vest before finally coming up with a few folded bills. "Here you go," he said while flicking the money at the barkeep. "Choke on it."

Like any man who'd become accustomed to dealing with an unruly public, the barkeep caught his money without getting cross at how it was delivered to him. "Much obliged, stranger."

"Come on, Adam," Mia said. "Time to go."

Adam accepted his sister's hand until he was solidly back on his feet. Then he shoved it away as if he hadn't needed it in the first place and resented the fact that it was so close to him. She'd also become accustomed to dealing with unruly drunks and walked to the door.

"I knew you didn't have it in you," he said.

The barkeep stooped down to pick up the spittoon that had been spattered with Adam's puke. Even after standing up again to survey the mess from higher ground, it took him a moment to realize Adam was looking at him. "I beg your pardon?"

"You heard me."

"Get out of my place before your sister needs to pull your fat from the fire again."

Adam punched the barkeep in the face. Even though his fist all but bounced off the other man's jaw without much more than a subtle smacking sound, he puffed out his chest and wore a vicious sneer when he said, "You didn't have the guts to finish me before, so why the hell would you do it now?"

Straightening up to stand several inches taller than Adam,

the barkeep held the ax handle so it was between both of their faces. "I don't beat on helpless drunks. Bad for repeat business."

Moving with speed that seemed impossible for someone in his condition, Adam grabbed the ax handle and jerked it away from its owner. He didn't even pause long enough to savor the astonishment on the barkeep's face before driving that length of lumber into his jaw.

"How about now?" Adam grunted. "Feel like stepping up to me now?"

"Beat his ass!" the old man shouted. Since neither of his eyes pointed in the same direction, it was impossible to say whether he was talking to Adam or the barkeep.

Mia had already stepped outside. She turned to look back into the saloon, but wasn't quick enough to realize how bad the situation was before it got even worse.

Adam took a cue from his sister when he snapped a knee straight up toward the barman's groin. The other man twisted just in time to take the hit on his hip, but that didn't help him any when it came to the ax handle, which dropped relentlessly down upon him.

"Come on, you piece of milk toast!" Adam said while hitting the barkeep with an intensity that grew with every blow. "Whose fat is in the fire now, huh? You don't even know, do you?"

"Adam! Stop it!" Mia pleaded. Like before, she was intent on getting to him no matter what was happening in his vicinity. Although he wasn't of a mind to harm her earlier, he wasn't thinking clearly enough to stop his swing before the ax handle clipped her on its way toward the barkeep. She dropped to the floor, which did nothing to slow Adam down.

The barkeep lowered his head, reached for the bar, and used it to pull himself up. As the insistent but weak blows continued bouncing off him, he calmly leaned across the warped wooden surface he'd spent so many hours wiping down and grabbed the sawed-off shotgun he kept for when things got really bad.

"That's right," Adam said as he gripped the ax handle with both fists. "Now you find your balls!"

"Adam, stop it!" Mia begged.

He pushed his sister back down, without even taking a moment to notice the blood on her skin.

When the barkeep wheeled around, he caught the ax handle after it bounced off his arm and pulled it to the side. Adam's fists remained in place as if they'd been glued to the dented length of wood. Rather than try to pull it away from the barkeep, he glared up at him while saying, "Your place is a shit hole and you smell like you were born at the bottom of the pile."

"Your bill's been paid," he replied. "Leave before I force you out."

"Force me how?"

Mia stepped up to him and placed a hand on his shoulder. "We're going. Right now!"

The barkeep held the shotgun at hip level, aiming at a spot that could cut Adam in half with the twitch of a trigger finger. His eyes snapped to Mia's hand, which was covered with a thin layer of blood that seeped into Adam's shirt. "Are you hurt, ma'am?"

She pulled her arm back and said, "It's nothing. We're leaving. Sorry about the inconvenience."

Adam looked at her hand and tracked the blood back to the minor cuts and scrapes that she'd collected while trying to pull him out of that saloon. "Go on, Mia," he said. "I'll be along shortly."

Nodding as if she was too tired to do much else, she turned and walked to the door.

"Go on, then, asshole," Adam said once he'd set his sights upon the barkeep once more. "Take care of your business while you still got the chance."

"Just get out of here," he replied.

"I'll be back to burn this pigsty to the ground."

"Will you, now?"

Taking a few more steps toward the bar, Adam nodded. "You best know I will. And if I have my way, you'll be in this shit hole when I light the torch."

Oddly enough, the two other customers in the place seemed more upset by that than the barkeep. They went to their spots and slammed their drinks back as if they truly had only a matter of seconds before it all went up in smoke.

The barkeep stood directly in front of Adam.

Mia stayed at the front door, holding it open as she said, "Come with me. *Now!*"

The closer the barkeep got, the more Adam seemed to sober up. The wildness in his eyes had died down, leaving a resolve that was more like rock at the base of a snow-capped mountain. "Go ahead and do it, you prick."

"You'd really like that, wouldn't you?"

Adam didn't say anything in response to the barkeep's question. He merely set his jaw and balled his fists in preparation for whatever was on its way.

The shotgun came up and was snapped around so the stock pounded against the side of Adam's head. It was a swift, brutally efficient move that came naturally to most saloon workers and lawmen. Adam's head snapped to one side and he dropped to the floor.

"He'll be all right, ma'am," the barkeep said to Mia. "When he wakes up, he'll just have a nasty headache, is all."

"I know," she sighed while trudging back into the place. "Could you help me get him out of here?"

"Just so long as he doesn't come back."

10

An hour after the sun rose the next morning, Slocum was up and ready to go. He was feeling the effects of a long night of playing cards, but had had enough distractions throughout the evening to keep his spirits up. When he knocked on the door to Mia's hotel room, the smell of coffee and frying bacon drifted up from the main floor.

"Where's your brother?" he asked after she pulled the door open. "The breakfast they're serving downstairs is calling my name."

"We'll be down before too long."

"What's the matter? Didn't you get enough rest last night?"

"No," she said with a cross tone. "I didn't. I tried to find you, but you weren't at your game. I went to your room and you weren't there. I asked around and all anyone could tell me was to look for someone named Natasha."

"Yeah, well, I suppose I did make the rounds last night," he said with a sheepish grin. "What did you need me for?"

Mia stepped aside and swept her hand toward the bed behind her. Adam lay there with an arm and leg dangling

78

off the side, wearing yesterday's clothes and a thick layer of bandages that had been wrapped around his head.

"What happened to him?" Slocum asked.

"He got drunk and started some trouble."

"Must have been in another saloon, because it sure wasn't in the place I was at." Slocum reached out to brush his hand along a bruised portion of her face. "What happened to you? Did he . . ."

Slocum didn't want to finish that question, but he didn't have to. The look of shame and sadness on her face told him more than enough.

"It was an accident," she told him. "He was starting a fight and I got too close when it was under way."

He nodded and glared at the man lying on the bed.

"Honestly, John. It was an accident."

"I heard you the first time. Do you want to get some breakfast?"

"What about you?" she asked.

"Why don't I save you the trouble of cleaning him up and loading him onto his horse? You go on ahead and have something to eat. If I'm not down there before you're finished, get something for me to eat once we're on the trail. We've still got a long ride ahead of us."

"It sounds like you had a good time last night, John. If you wanted to stay, we could take another day or two. Maybe Adam and I could move on by ourselves. You're a saint for bringing us this far."

"If it was just Adam, I'd leave him wherever he dropped the night before." Slocum brushed her hair back to check and see if there were any more wounds that she'd tried to cover up. As far as he could tell, there were only a few scrapes that very well could have happened just the way she'd described. Mia wasn't a lying sort, but she wouldn't have been the first to try and cover up for the missteps of a loved one.

Once it was obvious that he was searching for more

blood instead of just looking at her, Mia pushed his hand away and averted her eyes.

"Since it's the both of you traveling together," he continued, "I'll see to it that you get where you're going. Of course, since it looks like he may very well sleep for a while on his own, this'd be a good time for you to move on without him. I could take you to your family or even see you back to Bickell."

"I don't want to go back there," she said. "Not right away. I'll only have to deal with those men who were waiting for him before. He's my brother, after all. That means I need to see this through to the end."

"He's also a grown man. If any grown man would pick a fight and wake up with a bandaged head, he'd have to deal with it on his own. Trust me, I've been in that spot plenty of times."

Her smile was an even pleasanter sight than the rising sun. Her rounded cheeks flushed and her soft eyes crinkled at the edges as she quickly tried to cover the fact that she'd been ready to giggle at him. "I just bet you have."

"I never had someone like you to scrape me off the floor, though. Did you ever think that maybe he needs to stay on the floor sometimes? You might be surprised how a man can change when he sees things from down there for a while."

The humor that had briefly shown on her face quickly disappeared. "He's been down there plenty," she said. "I can't bear to leave him there anymore." She placed a hand on his chest and tried to keep him from entering the room, but Slocum planted his feet once he was inside and wouldn't be shooed away.

"I'll get him cleaned up," he said. "You get some breakfast. At least that way he won't have the indignity of having his sister changing his britches."

"Nothing I haven't had to do plenty of times already, but it's not something I look forward to." She drew a breath and then let it out with a curt nod. "All right. I'll get breakfast and arrange for the horses."

"Ed's already collecting the horses. Just have something to eat. I'll bring your brother and things down as soon as I'm able."

"Thank you, John. I really appreciate it."

When she reached up to place her hand on his cheek, it seemed to come as a surprise to her. Mia's smile returned and she patted him affectionately. He nodded, stepped aside so she could leave the room, and then closed the door behind her. Only after he'd heard her steps echo far enough down the hall did he turn around to face the bed.

"That you, Mia?" Adam groaned.

Slocum double-checked to make sure the door was locked.

Adam pulled in half a breath, hacked it up, and rubbed his face. When his hands brushed against the bloodied spots on his temple and jaw, he hissed and covered his eyes with his arm. "Bring me some water, would ya?"

There was a water basin on a table between the door and the bed, so Slocum walked over there and picked it up.

"I feel like hell," Adam said. "How long was I sleepin'?"

Slocum didn't answer, which didn't seem to bother Adam in the slightest. He just kept on talking with his eyes covered and his leg hanging off the side of the bed.

"No need to spout off about what happened in that saloon, I already know what you're gonna say."

"Do you?"

The sound of Slocum's voice instead of his sister's was enough of a surprise to get him to sit up straight. At least, his body tried to straighten before fatigue, his injuries, and last night's whiskey stopped him short. "Oh," he said while lowering his head back onto the pillow. "It's you."

"Get up."

"Why don't you get out?"

"You heard what I said," Slocum growled. "Don't make me say it again."

"This is my room, damn it. And I say to—"

Adam must have still been a little drunk, because Slocum figured any man with a working set of eyes would have known that the water basin in his hands wasn't meant for a sponge bath. Even so, he dumped its contents onto Adam's head with no small amount of satisfaction.

"What the hell?" Adam sputtered as he thrashed on the bed and fought to wipe the water from his face.

"You'll get up," Slocum demanded, "and you'll collect you and your sister's things so we can have a proper breakfast and be out of here."

"Who are you now? My pappy?"

"I ain't your pappy, your brother, or even your friend. The only reason I don't drown you in one of the puddles I just made is on account of your sister."

"Oh, you like her, do you? Well, you can have her."

Slocum smashed the water basin against the headboard inches above Adam's scalp. Pieces were still raining down when Slocum grabbed him by the front of his shirt and hauled him out of the bed. "Get to your feet, you prissy little cur."

"Who're you callin' a—"

Too impatient to wait for Adam to get his words out, Slocum pulled him close and snarled directly into his face. "I'm talking to you and I meant every damn word! We've listened to you cry and moan for days so now it's your turn."

Adam tried to squirm away, but Slocum's grip was much too solid for him to break.

"I heard you had a little misadventure last night while Ed and I were playing cards."

"Playing cards or fuckin' some whore?"

Slocum shook Adam so hard that some of his teeth may have rattled loose. He hadn't meant to be so rough, but

Adam hung from his fists like a wet rag doll rather than put up any sort of fight. "You don't have the right to judge anyone, you hear?"

"I hear plenty," Adam grunted.

"Good, because I want you to hear this and think real closely before you answer. You wanna die?"

"Huh?"

"Do you want to die?"

Adam blinked once and smirked. "Ain't you heard? I'm already dead."

"Dead men don't cause this much trouble for their families," Slocum said. "And ghosts don't stink nearly as much as you do right now. So that means you must like playing dead. If that's all you want, then find a soft bed somewhere, roll over like a good dog, and play dead. You've put your sister through enough hell."

"My whole life ain't nothin' but hell, mister."

"Yeah, I heard about that. You're real sick. Nobody knows what's wrong. You hurt. You ache. Poor little baby. You still haven't answered my question, Adam. Do you want to die?" When he got nothing but a hateful glare from the wobbly man, Slocum said, "I've known a few men who were wracked with illness. Some of them tried to live out their lives the best they could and some wanted to wring as much out of this world as possible before their short time in it ran out. Those men usually wind up being some crazy bastards, but they're worth knowing."

Slocum allowed Adam to get the first hint of a grin on his face before adding, "You're not one of those men. You're a pathetic little toad who's too yellow to either grab the bull by the horns or do himself in properly." He let go of Adam with a shove that bounced him once more against the headboard.

Slapping at the bed and the wooden headboard in angry frustration, Adam flopped off the other side and then stomped around it to stand before Slocum. "You don't even know me! How dare you act like you know what I've been through!"

"I may not know where you've been, but I've seen enough to know where you are. There's plenty men out in the world who are worse off than you and they don't spend every day of their miserable lives trying to get someone to put a bullet through their skulls."

"What would you have me do? Raise some cows? Start up a dry goods store?"

"I don't give a damn what you do, but if you had a scrap of honor, you wouldn't torture a good woman like your sister the way you do."

"Did she tell you about our mother? She wasted away inside a locked room because of this sickness that's got me. Our father did his best to carry on the way he always did and he wasted away just the same. I ain't about to spend my few remaining years like that!"

"So you do want to die," Slocum said.

"It's not my choice, but it's what I got comin' my way."

"That's comin' for all of us sooner or later."

"Sure," Adam said, "but not everyone gets to look the reaper in the face every goddamn second of every goddamn day."

"You certain about that?"

A quick response came to Adam's lips, but didn't make it past them. The cold look in Slocum's eyes was more than enough to make him think twice about the next words he spoke. Finally, he turned his back to him and started collecting his clothes from a pile beside the bed. "I've seen what sickness can do to people and I don't want that."

"You'd rather go down in a whole mess of loud words, blood, and gunfire, huh?"

"Maybe," Adam replied while slipping into the same clothes he'd worn the day before. "Anything wrong with that?"

"Only when some of that gunfire spills the wrong people's blood. Your sister looks like she was the one in the fight. How do you come to terms with that?"

Shrugging, Adam buttoned his shirt and said, "I told her to leave me alone. She should've done that."

"You don't care if she got hurt because of you?"

"Sure I do, but she didn't get shot."

Slocum nodded as he picked up one of the saddlebags lying against the table where the washbasin had been. When he turned around, he tossed the bag so it hit Adam squarely in the chest. The impact wasn't enough to knock him down, but it put Adam off his balance while Slocum rushed up to him and said, "This is your lucky day, friend, because I'm sick of hearing your tough talk and sad stories. You want to die in a blaze of gunfire?" he asked while drawing the Colt Navy from its holster. "Here's your chance."

Although Adam put on a shaky grin, he couldn't maintain it when Slocum grabbed his wrist so he could slap the Colt's handle against his palm. "What's this?"

"It's a pistol, Adam," Slocum said while closing the other man's fingers around the Colt's grip. "I would have thought you'd know that by now. Since you seem to have forgotten where yours is during all of these sorrowful and lonely times, perhaps you'd like to use mine?"

"What?"

"Just trying to do you a favor. You know what they say. If you want a job done right, you have to do it yourself. Tell you what. If you screw this up like you've done with everything else so far, I'll be sure and finish it. Is that what's got you shaking so hard right now? You worried you might just blast off the bottom of your jaw or tear off your face? I promise I won't let you suffer. Anything like that happens and I'll send you right to the Promised Land in the space of a few heartbeats."

Sweat broke out upon Adam's brow and trickled down his cheek. It dripped off the tip of his nose and pattered against the floor when he started shaking his head vehemently. "I don't want this. I want to . . ."

"You want to what?" Slocum growled. "Die with your boots on?"

The motion of Adam's head changed directions from a shake to a nod. "Better that than waste away slowly like . . . like . . ."

"Like the rest of us?"

Adam blinked, and when he looked at Slocum again, it was as if he'd finally woken up.

"Not all of us may have your cough or aches or whatever the hell you've got," Slocum said. "To tell you the truth, apart from you being drunk and looking a little green behind the gills sometimes, I wouldn't have even guessed you were that sick."

"That's why I'm drunk most of the time," Adam said. "Feels better that way."

"If that's what makes you feel better, then drink your whiskey. It ain't like you're the only one pouring firewater down their throats whenever they get the chance. Answer one question, though. What do you think it means to die with your boots on?"

Scowling as though he'd just been asked to explain why the dirt was brown, Adam said, "It means dying standing up, out in the world, kicking up dust and raring to go until someone puts you down."

"Sounds pretty good to me. How about you start *living* that way?"

Adam's eyes drifted away from Slocum, but they seemed to be focused upon something that wasn't even in the room. He shook his head slowly and was almost no longer able to remain on his own two feet. "Here," he said while handing the Colt back. "Take it."

"You sure? If you still want to die, I could do it real quick and still be done in time for breakfast."

"Best take it before I use it to shut your smart mouth up for good," Adam said with a tired scowl.

Slocum took the Colt, holstered it, and then headed for the door. "I hope I got through that hard skull of yours."

"You did."

"Good. Just don't mistake that as anything too friendly. As long as we're on the same trail, I don't want to have to deal with this kind of idiotic bullshit anymore, you hear?"

"Yes," Adam sighed.

"Now collect all of your things, bring them downstairs, and get the horses loaded. We've got a long few days ahead of us."

11

As they rode past Dallas, Slocum could feel anxious eyes pointed in his direction. Even Mia cleared her throat as they rode past the fork in the road that would take them back into civilization.

"Nope," was all Slocum said as he flicked his reins and led them onward.

Since nobody was about to argue or strike out on their own, the entire group kept going.

Slocum found it amusing how he'd become the leader of the expedition. It wasn't as if New Orleans was hard to find. Mia and Adam simply wanted to get into Louisiana, where they had family waiting for them, so they should have been able to find their way on their own. As for Triedle's motives, those had been made clear from the start. Since they'd ridden away from Darnell with more money in their pockets than when they'd arrived, those motives had become set in stone.

By the time Dallas was behind them, Slocum's mind was another day's ride ahead. He thought about different paths he might take, different towns he might visit, and different tribes they might encounter along the way. The Indians weren't much of a problem so long as they were approached properly. Some of them, however, were as savage as the land they claimed as their own.

"You know, Dallas is a great town," Triedle called out from his spot at the back of the line.

"So I've heard," Slocum replied.

"Plenty of saloons."

"Yep."

"Some real good gambling halls. There was a fire that burned down a section of the gaming district, and the places that were put up afterward are even better than the first."

"I suppose that's what they call progress."

"Yeah!" Triedle said. "How about we see it for ourselves?"

Slocum waited to hear Adam chime in with his plea to visit a saloon. When it didn't come, he turned around to see if Mia's brother had fallen from his saddle without anyone noticing. But Adam was right where he should have been. In response to Slocum's backward glance, he merely shrugged and coughed into the bandanna that was wrapped around his fist.

"We keep going," Slocum said as he shifted to face forward again. "We're not on a tour of card tables."

"Speak for yourself," Triedle grumbled.

"You wanna ride ahead?"

Even though he couldn't see him, Slocum could picture the look of glee that was on Triedle's face when he shouted back, "Hell yes I do!"

"Then ride on ahead and scout to make sure the trail's clear. It's been a long time since I've ridden this way and we should make sure I'm not taking us to a washed-out bridge or something else that'll only cost us daylight."

"Aw, to hell with you."

"You think I'm kidding?" Slocum asked sternly.

Like any dutiful soldier, Triedle snapped his reins and

rode ahead while muttering very uncomplimentary things under his breath.

"That was impressive," Mia said once Triedle had ridden too far away to hear her. "Is this a dangerous trail?"

"No. I just didn't think he'd go."

Her laugh grew louder as Mia spurred her horse just enough to catch up to Slocum's. Once she'd drawn even with him, she rode quietly for a spell. Slocum looked over at her and couldn't help but admire the way the sunlight kissed the swooping curls of her hair and brought a red hue to her cheeks and neck. He noticed a subtle upward tilt to her nose, which made her face look like it was always in the process of smiling.

After looking quickly over her shoulder, she leaned toward Slocum and whispered, "What did you say to Adam back at the hotel?"

"Not much."

"Did you hit him?"

Slocum twitched as if that question had reached out to flick him on the nose. "Did I what?"

"Well, it had to have been something drastic," she said while taking a gander back at her brother, who was slouching forward and half asleep in his saddle. "Nothing I've ever been able to do has made a dent. So I guess I thought—"

"You thought I'd be the one to dent him," Slocum said. "It's always nice to see how other folks look at you."

"I don't think badly of you, John. It's just that he's different now. Quieter."

"I know. Makes for a nice ride. Now that we're rid of Ed for a little while, we should enjoy it."

She was quieter, too, having lowered her voice so it didn't carry so easily back to the topic of conversation. "I'm serious. What happened after I left that hotel room? Adam hasn't been the same since he told me to go to hell when I woke him up."

"Just let him be," Slocum said, even though he couldn't

believe those words had come out of his mouth. "The last thing he needs is you coddling him."

"Someone has to."

"No. They don't. He's a grown man, not a sick puppy."

She smiled at him in a way that made the whole day seem warmer. "John Slocum, if I didn't know any better, I'd say you give a damn about my brother."

"Good thing you know better."

But she wasn't about to swallow that. Mia continued smiling, unaffected by the edge in his voice.

"You seem awfully happy," Slocum said.

"Things are just turning out better than I'd hoped."

"Well, try to keep your spirits high. It seems our peace and quiet is about finished."

Following his line of sight, Mia quickly spotted the dust being kicked up by Triedle's horse. At first, she thought it was him scouting ahead. Then she realized he was on his way back.

"Damn," Slocum sighed. "Figured he'd at least stay away for a while longer."

"Be nice. He's your friend."

"Since when?"

Even if Triedle had heard this exchange, he wouldn't have been affected by it. He was too busy waving his arm and snapping his reins to be bothered with any words that passed between Slocum and Mia. Once he got close enough to be heard over the thunder of his horse's hooves, he started speaking in a rush that was so quick it might as well have been a gust of wind coming from his mouth.

"Slow down!" Slocum said. "What's got you so riled up?"

Triedle took a breath, acknowledged the two of them with a nod, and then said, "There's a group of horses over that ridge."

"Anything more than that or were you expecting everyone else in Texas to clear a path for us?"

"They're waiting for us."

Mia gasped and Slocum tried to calm her with a hand placed upon her elbow. "How do you know they're waiting for us?" he asked.

"Because that's what they told me to tell you."

Slocum stared daggers at the gambler, trying to think of a way to convey how fed up he was with this conversation and how close he was to ending it with a few quick shots from his Colt. That look accomplished the task because Triedle forced himself to start over while moving his horse around to fall into step on Slocum's left.

"It's Cale and two others. Wasn't he the fella that was waiting for Mia and Adam outside her house?"

"Yes," Mia said.

Sitting bolt upright in his saddle, Adam drew up close to the other three horses and asked, "Did you say Cale Terrigan is waiting for us?"

"Am I still messing up my words?" Triedle snapped. "Yes, that's what I said and they're just over that ridge. I saw them as soon as I crested it and they signaled me to come over and have a word with them."

"You were barely gone long enough for any of this to happen," Slocum said.

Before Triedle could respond to that, three men on horseback slowly rode over the ridge directly ahead of them. They stopped once they were at the top of the gently sloping rise, as if that little bit of high ground gave them every tactical advantage in the world.

"Howdy," Cale said with a wave. "We didn't think we were gonna catch up to you. That is, until you did us the favor of stopping off in Darnell. Appreciate the chance to have this chat with you."

"I see you found a man to replace the one you lost," Slocum said. "Hopefully you told him what happened to that other one."

"I sure did. Don't worry about that. In fact, since both of

these men knew Paul, they were more than willing to help me come after you."

"Paul?"

"My brother," Cale said. "The one that you killed."

Adam rode forward until he was ahead of Slocum, but not quite up to where Triedle had come to a stop. "If you're after payback, then look to me for it. I'm the reason all of this business with you was dredged up in the first place."

"Don't need to remind me of that," Cale replied. "But it ain't just about you anymore. It's about all of you. The way I see it, any one of you could have ended things better. Instead, you had to shortchange me and light a fire under the whole situation."

"You were the ones waiting for us back at that house," Slocum said. "Or did you forget?"

Cale shot back with, "I was waiting to collect on a debt I was owed."

"Which we negotiated until you decided to grab for more!"

"Only half settled. Not even that. And that's just the money portion. There's a blood debt now and I intend on collecting every bit of it."

The three men fanned out. All of them had their guns drawn, but weren't making a show of it. Still, something didn't seem right.

"There's two more," Triedle whispered. "I spotted 'em on the way back here."

Slocum nodded, accepting that as precisely the sort of thing that had been making him uneasy. "You'll have the rest of your money when we get back to Bickell," he said to Cale.

The gunman shook his head. "That ain't good enough. You already ran this far. You think I'm stupid enough to believe you'll just turn around and come back to pay me?"

"Our home is back there," Mia said. "We sure aren't dragging everything we own on the backs of these horses."

A wicked smile oozed onto Cale's face as he said, "You're right about that. I might even go so far as to say that you won't be carrying much of anything on them horses. Why don't you hand 'em over as part of your payment?"

"And we're supposed to believe that you'll just take some horses as a way to make up for what happened to your brother?" Slocum asked. "We're not stupid either, you know."

"Maybe not, but there ain't a lot you can do about it. Hand 'em over."

"John, those other two could be anywhere," Triedle warned.

"You're sure there were only two?"

"No. I came back as fast as I could to tell you what was happening. You think I should have lagged behind to count heads?"

"Might have been helpful," Slocum snapped.

Cale allowed the back and forth between them to continue for a few seconds, still grinning as if it was part of the day's entertainment. Before long, he said, "I'll take your horse for now, Adam. Seems fair considering you're the one who owes me the money."

"No," Slocum said while extending an arm toward Adam. Although his arm wasn't long enough to reach him, the gesture alone stopped Adam in his tracks. Slocum kept his eyes on the men in front of him as he said, "You tried this before and were barely able to get out alive. You got all the money we can spare for now and will get the rest later. That was the deal."

"I didn't agree to no deal."

"The hell you didn't!" Mia snapped.

Despite the surprise of hearing that tone in her voice, Slocum didn't take his eyes off Cale and his men. "You'd best think twice about what you're doing here," he said. "And if you get any bright ideas, think again about how things turned out last time. It's a shame anyone had to die, but things could have been a whole lot worse. Turn back and go about your business. You'll get your payment when we come back to Bickell."

The gunman nodded solemnly and took a deep breath. He made a big show of rubbing his chin and drumming his fingers, but wasn't fooling anyone. Still, they all waited to see what he would come up with next. Finally, Cale said, "You're right. I think I will be on my way."

Cale pulled his reins to steer his horse all the way around to face the opposite direction. The men beside him did the same and all three of them moved away. After taking a few steps, he held up his arm and tossed a casual wave in Slocum's direction.

Slocum wasn't about to count his blessings for resolving the situation, but before he could assess the situation, a horse's snuffing breath drifted from the left of the trail. Slocum turned to look and found a rifleman sitting there, mostly hidden behind a cluster of trees. He was already sighting along the top of his weapon, so Slocum shouted, "Scatter!"

A shot cracked through the air, hissing through the space where Slocum and the others had been. It was impossible to tell who the rifleman was aiming for, but he didn't hit anyone. That didn't deter him from levering another round and taking aim. In the time that took, Slocum had drawn his Colt and fired two quick shots at the trees. The rifleman sent his next round hastily across the trail, whipping close enough to Mia to make her scream.

Despite the situation, Slocum grew calmer once he'd gotten his horse under control. It was a good animal and wasn't the kind to get skittish at loud noises or gunfire. The other horses were doing well enough to keep his line of fire clear for the few seconds he needed to steady his aim. He squeezed his trigger once and then again just to be sure, but knew the second bullet wasn't necessary.

He was right for the most part. The rifleman grunted and

reeled back in his saddle, but shots kept coming from Triedle and Adam, who'd skinned their pistols and returned fire. According to the gambler's attempt at scouting, there was still at least one other gunman unaccounted for. Thinking back to Cale's previous tactics, Slocum turned around to look at the opposite side of the trail to see if anyone meant to flank him from there. Sure enough, another rifleman was there but hadn't had a chance to get in a good position and Slocum wasn't about to give him a chance to do so. He fired toward that rider, causing him to duck down low and keep moving before he was picked off.

A few shots came from Cale's direction, which was where Triedle and Adam now concentrated their fire. Suddenly, the first rifleman sent a round at Slocum that was too low to hit him. The bullet slapped into his horse's side and was followed by another. The animal shuddered beneath him, staggering to one side, and tried to whinny but couldn't push the sound up from the back of its throat. Knowing the horse was about to fall, Slocum jumped from the saddle before he was trapped under its weight. He was just quick enough to avoid getting crushed as the horse dropped to one front knee and then keeled over. As if to wipe away any question about his intent, the rifleman levered in another round and sent it straight into the wounded horse's neck.

"How you like that, Slocum?" Cale shouted from a distance. "I got the horse I wanted after all!"

"You'll get more than that!" Slocum bellowed as he tried to pull his rifle from the saddle's boot. Unfortunately, that was the side the horse had landed and he had to pull with all of his strength before the rifle would even budge.

"We'll be along shortly for the rest of what you owe," Cale yelled. "I'll let you stew about the where and when."

"Stew nothin'!" Slocum hollered. "We'll settle this now!"

Cale laughed loudly, not seeming to mind the gunshots

that blazed around him. Even though his men were trading shots with Adam and Triedle, nobody was able to line anything up that drew much blood. They were just a bunch of men pulling their triggers too quickly instead of keeping calm and sighting properly.

By the time Slocum managed to pull the rifle out from under his horse, the rifleman he'd knocked from his saddle was being helped back up again by another of Cale's men. "That's right!" Slocum shouted as he took aim. "I ain't through with you yet!"

Slocum's shot was hasty and resulted in a large section of bark getting ripped from a tree. The gunman coming to the rifleman's aid fired once to cover himself until his partner was on his feet. Holding the rifle against his shoulder, Slocum walked toward them and lined up his shot properly.

"John, look out!"

Not paying any mind to the warning, Slocum shouted an obscenity at the two gunmen in his sights and squeezed his trigger. Just as his rifle's hammer dropped, something pounded into his side. Everything toppled around him before he hit the ground with an impact that drove the breath from his lungs. He demanded an explanation from whoever had knocked him down, but his words were drowned out by the crackle of gunshots that came in from farther down the trail.

"I told you to look out," Triedle said as he rushed over to help him up. "Now keep your head down, for Christ's sake!"

"Get off'a me!"

The gambler wasn't about to fight with him, so he rolled away. In the trees, both of Cale's men were trying to make good on their escape but Slocum dropped one of them with another carefully aimed shot.

Adam remained in his saddle, screaming Cale's name

at the trees or anything else in front of him as he fired until his old .44 ran dry. After a few loud slaps of the pistol's hammer hitting spent bullet casings, he reloaded without paying any mind to the shots that were still hissing by.

"Adam!" Mia shouted from where she was huddled against a half-buried rock. "Watch yourself!"

But Adam didn't budge. He finished what he was doing, closed up the .44, and fired at the trees where the two men that Slocum had targeted had been. When he saw that spot was vacant, he flicked his reins to set out after Cale and the others.

"Adam, no! Come back."

Although he'd ignored everything else until then, he wasn't about to let that plea go unanswered. He fired a few shots toward the rise where Cale's voice had originated while steering his horse around to face his sister. Even as he settled in a position to put himself between him and any incoming bullets, he was still firing his pistol.

Triedle stood up and dusted himself off. "Enough! All of you!" He seemed more surprised than anyone when the firing stopped. "That's better. Can't you see they've gone?"

"Give me your horse," Slocum demanded.

"They're not there anymore, John. They—"

"Give me your horse!"

"You've been shot, for Christ's sake!"

Slocum felt the aching spot on his hip. There was blood coming from a wound there, but the bullet had done more damage to his jeans and gun belt than to his body. Denim and leather had been chewed away and blackened, revealing a shallow groove carved into his flesh. "I'm fine."

"John, you need to—"

Slocum cut Triedle off by pointing the rifle at him.

"I'm no stranger to calling a bluff," the gambler said.

Slocum narrowed his eyes to angry slits and levered in a fresh round.

"Maybe not bluffing," Triedle said. "All right, then. Help yourself." When Slocum grabbed the reins from him and climbed onto the horse's back, Triedle shouted, "You're welcome!"

12

Slocum returned a few minutes later. Several minutes ago, the spot had been just another stretch of trail on the long way to Louisiana. Now, it looked like a section of a battlefield that had been cut off from the whole like a hunk of bloody pie. Smoke hung in the air, blood stained the dirt, and a woman's muffled sobs could be heard beneath a restless wind.

"Did you find anything else to shoot?" Triedle asked.

Eyeing the gambler intently, Slocum replied, "Maybe."

Triedle backed off.

The horse lying on the ground was still trembling. Most of the blood on the ground seemed to come from its wounds, but Slocum checked the others to be sure. Mia was unharmed and Adam had caught a few glancing rounds that had ripped through his upper arm without doing a whole lot of damage.

"You're lucky," Mia told her brother. "I still can't believe you're not dead."

Adam pressed a hand against the wound on his arm and said, "Yeah. Real lucky."

"I'm fine, by the way," Triedle offered. "Not that anyone seems to care."

Slocum dismounted and threw his reins at the gambler. "Obviously you're fine," he said. "You're up and moving, aren't you?"

"I suppose, but still. A little concern would be nice."

"Are you all right?" Slocum asked.

Triedle smiled and nodded once. "Yes, I am."

"Good. Now stop your bellyaching." Slocum's eyes were already on the horse. His face twisted into an angry mask beneath a thick layer of dust and gunpowder that had drifted onto him and mingled with the sweat on his skin.

Mia stepped forward and placed a hand upon Slocum's shoulder. "Are you hurt?" she asked.

He shook away from her and winced in pain as he knelt beside the wounded animal. A quick inspection was all he needed to surmise that the wounds were grievous enough to keep it from getting up from where it had fallen. "Those sons of bitches." Patting the side of the horse's face, he added, "Fucking animals will pay for this."

Even though Slocum's touch was gentle, the horse trembled as if it could feel the impact of his hand all the way down to its belly. Without letting another moment of suffering go by, Slocum stood up, drew his pistol, and put a single round through the horse's head. It shuddered once more and let out a breath that allowed its body to finally rest peacefully. When he looked up, Slocum's expression made it clear that he was searching for a better place to send his next round.

"What do we do now?" Mia asked sheepishly.

"I'm surprised you haven't taken another horse and gone after those assholes," Triedle said.

"They've got a lead on us after riling us up and ambushing us once already," Slocum pointed out. "And that's after they tracked us this far, which means they can track us again. From the sound of what Cale said when he left, he intends on setting up another ambush somewhere along the line. Charging off after them right now sounds like a damn fine idea."

"I didn't say it was a good idea. I just said I was surprised you hadn't gone after them yet."

Slocum looked at Adam, but his eyes settled firmly on Mia. "That's just what he wants from us, so that's the last thing we should give him."

"If you're holding back on account of me, don't bother," she said. "I'll do anything you need for us to put those dogs down for good."

Although he admired her spirit, Slocum wasn't about to take advantage of it just to appease the anger that still raged inside him. When he thought about playing into Cale's hands, it seemed more and more likely that the main purpose of this ambush had been to set up a second one. For all he knew, there was another set of riflemen positioned along the trail just waiting for a clean shot.

"We'll get our chance," he said once the fire in his gut had finally dwindled a bit. "We'll take it on our time, is all. I doubt those men will simply ride off and not come back."

Mia looked relieved to hear that and the other two were just happy to get moving. Slocum wanted to get away from the horse carcass, even though it didn't seem right to just leave it there. On the other hand, it seemed even less right to spend more time than necessary lollygagging in the spot where they'd already been bushwhacked.

They were down a horse, so Slocum emptied his saddlebags and divided his things among what little extra space there was in the other packs. After tying a makeshift bandage over his flesh wound, he retrieved all of his belongings, switched out Mia's saddle for his own, and climbed onto that horse's back.

"So that's the way it's going to be?" she asked as he offered a hand down to her. "My horse is the one you take?"

"I'm not taking it for good. We've got to keep riding, don't we?"

"Yes, but—"

"Just climb up here so we can go!" When Mia still shuffled her feet in getting over to him, Slocum looked to Adam and asked, "Has she always been this difficult?"

"She's never been able to ride behind someone on a horse, I can tell you that much," he replied. "Ever since we were kids, she was always falling off."

"All right, enough of this," she said. Mia grabbed Slocum's hand and nearly pulled him down in her haste to climb up. "Here. Happy now?"

"Just sit still and hang on tight." As soon as her arms were wrapped around him from behind, Slocum added, "That's it. Now I'm happy."

She grumbled something under her breath, but didn't loosen her grip. With a flick of the reins, he got her horse moving again. It took several paces for the animal to adjust to the added weight, but found its stride quickly enough.

"There's another trail we can use a few miles away," Slocum announced. "That still leaves plenty of room for a trap to be sprung, but if I remember correctly, it's mostly open country between here and there. We should be all right so long as we keep our eyes peeled."

"I'll take the lead," Adam said.

Slocum watched him trot forward from the back where he'd ridden most of the time so far. "You sure about that?" he asked.

"Yeah," Adam replied while reloading his old .44.

Normally, Slocum wouldn't be too happy about putting a man with a death wish in charge of spotting potential danger. But there was something different about Adam now. A glint of life was in his eyes that had only gotten stronger when Mia had been forced to hide amid a storm of gunfire. Whether Adam was still riled up from the ambush or if he'd had a genuine change of heart, he seemed to be the perfect man for the job. He only lacked one thing.

"Here," Slocum said while tossing over his rifle. "You'll need this if you intend on hitting anything before they can hit us. Do you know how to use one of those things?"

"Adam won four sharpshooting contests," Mia said proudly.

"Is that true?"

"Yeah," Adam said. "When I was ten. I still know my way around a rifle, though. It's not like they've changed which end the bullet comes from."

"He's amusing when he's not sulking," Triedle said. "I'll bring up the rear."

The three horses rode in single file over the rise. Every step of the way, Slocum waited for a shot to be fired at them or for someone to try and ride up close enough to do some damage with a pistol or shotgun. Rather than try to figure out exactly what might happen, he did his best to be ready for anything. They rode at a steady trot, moving quickly toward the spot where they could switch trails without going fast enough for them to play into Cale's hands. Although they twitched at the sounds of a few birds getting flushed from some bushes, they didn't find anything worth their trouble.

A single shot cracked through the air. As Slocum's hand snapped onto the grip of his Colt, one of the birds dropped from the sky.

"There we go," Adam said while levering a fresh round into Slocum's rifle. "Is that enough for supper, or should I look for more?"

"How about you wait until we're not so worried about giving away our position?" Slocum asked.

"Sorry about that."

Adam was anxious to either prove himself or dust off his sharpshooting skills because he almost fired another shot at some rabbits that darted across the trail. After they'd stopped long enough for Adam to collect the bird he'd shot, they picked up their pace and headed east.

Every so often, Slocum would slow the group to take a look through the field glasses that had fortunately not been crushed by his wounded horse. He surveyed the terrain while craning his neck and doing his level best to look behind every tree. As near as he could tell, Cale and his boys had moved on and weren't interested in charging them just yet. Either that, or they were good enough to shadow them without being spotted. Neither choice mattered much because Slocum still had to keep moving and wouldn't let his guard down either way.

The other trail Slocum had in mind was an overgrown set of wagon ruts that could have easily been mistaken for simple grooves cut into the dirt by an old stream or a fence that had been pulled up or blown away years ago. Slocum was extra careful in making the switch from one trail to the other. If Cale or one of his men spotted them at the wrong time, the effort of changing routes would lose its purpose.

Adam rode ahead until he found a good patch of high ground that allowed him to scout for anyone tracking them without making him easy to see from a distance. Slocum steered Mia's horse off the trail, following it in a parallel path as if he was looking for a good spot to answer the call of nature. Every so often, he would angle away a little farther while keeping those overgrown ruts in his sights. Triedle stayed behind, lagging farther and farther to watch for anyone who'd circled around to get at them from that angle. So far, the only thing behind any of the riders was the dust kicked up by their horses.

Once Slocum was on the alternate trail, he rode slowly until the other two drifted in to fall back into their previous formation. The riding slowed down considerably, mainly because of the state of the trail itself. Although it was relatively easy to follow after riding on it for a while, the ground was uneven, the dirt was filled with rocks, and old trees had fallen down as if purposely trying to trip up any animals dumb enough to continue along that path.

"How many days are we tacking on to the ride with this little diversion?" Triedle asked. Although he'd been the only one to speak up, it was obvious that everyone else was anxious to hear Slocum's answer.

"Maybe two," he said. "But there's an advantage to going this way. We're saving time we would have spent skirting through some swampland that ain't particularly kind to the nose. Also, there should be a town ahead."

"How far?"

"Normally, I'd say we'd reach it tomorrow. But I think we might be able to get there with just a little bit of night riding if we set our minds to it and made sure not to dawdle."

Although the Weylands seemed to be pleased with that news, Triedle wasn't so quick to celebrate. "And you're sure this isn't just a carrot you're dangling in front of us?" he asked.

"I beg your pardon?"

"You're the worst taskmaster I've ever ridden with. I'm just making sure there's really a town and that it's not just something you can use to make us ride faster without talking or doing anything else to ruffle your feathers for another day."

"And what was I supposed to do at the end of the day if there ain't no town?" Slocum asked.

"Simple. You say you were mistaken and that it must be a little further up the road or on some other godforsaken busted trail that's stuck away in the back of your head so we keep going. Sooner or later, we'd come across a settlement and you could say that's the one you were thinking of."

Even though such tactics had sprung to mind more than once since they'd all stricken out from Bickell, Slocum said, "I am offended you'd say such a thing, Ed. And after all the ground we've covered as partners."

"Partners, my ass," Triedle squawked. "It was damn close to pullin' teeth just to get you to sit down to a card table until we were already ahead by a hundred dollars."

"All right, then," Slocum said. "You're so fond of gambling. If you're certain that I'm full of shit, then put your money where your mouth is!"

"There's no need for that," Mia said while patting his shoulder.

But Slocum would have none of it. "Come on, Ed. You think I'm a liar? Back it up."

"I never said you were a liar," Triedle explained. "I believe the word I used was 'taskmaster.'"

"That's the word," Adam said from the front of the line. "I heard it."

"I suppose it's an honest mistake," Slocum said through gritted teeth. "Especially since the fact that you questioned me at all the way you did means you think I'd lie to all of your faces. All this after I nearly got shot trying to run off that asshole Cale."

"Aw, Cale's not even after us," Triedle said dismissively. "He's after them other two."

"Honestly, all of you," Mia said in a louder voice than the one she'd used before. "None of this is getting us anywhere."

"You know what's not getting us anywhere?" Triedle asked. "This goddamned trail!"

Slocum pulled back on his reins, bringing his horse to a stop so quickly that he almost forced Triedle's to walk straight into him. "That's it! Off yer horse. Right now!"

Mia's hand tightened on his shoulder, as if she thought she could hold him in place as she said, "That's enough. We've got a lot of ground to cover and we won't get to that town if we stop to bicker amongst ourselves."

"Don't worry," Triedle said. "Bickering for a while won't matter because there isn't a town!"

Slocum brushed Mia's hand from his shoulder and swung

down from the saddle. "Get down here right now, or by God, I'll pull you down."

Triedle swiped at the beads of sweat that rolled down his face. "Just get back on your horse and lead the way, O fearless trailsman."

"We really should keep moving," Adam said.

"See, John? Don't you feel foolish when a sickly fool like that is the voice of reason?"

That caused Adam to look at Triedle with almost enough fire in his eyes to match Slocum's. "What did you call me?"

"Oh, don't bother denying it," the gambler said. "Just sit up there and sulk like always."

"He's been making himself more useful than you," Slocum said while stabbing a finger up at Triedle. "Now get down from your horse."

"Yeah," Adam said after reining his horse to a stop so he could climb down from its back. "Maybe you should do what he says."

"All of you just simmer down," Mia demanded. "It's been a rough day and we're all not in the best frame of mind."

"Just shut up and keep to your own affairs," Triedle snapped.

Adam shoved past Slocum in his haste to approach the gambler's horse. "Don't talk to her like that!"

When he was knocked aside, Slocum retaliated by shoving Adam back.

"Don't test me," Adam said. "Especially not after being taunted by a cheating little prick like that."

Since he was being singled out by Adam's pointing finger, Triedle growled, "Cheating? You call me a cheater?" He swung one leg over his horse's back and slipped his other from the stirrup just enough to use it as a launching point so he could throw himself down onto both Adam and Slocum. He bounced off of one to land on the other. Because of the way he spread out his arms and legs, kicking and flailing like a crazed hawk swooping down for a mouse, it was difficult for Mia to see which man got the worst of it.

"Stop it," she pleaded. "What are you doing?"

But her words fell upon deaf ears. The other three men either weren't listening or were too busy getting their faces punched to notice someone was talking.

"You called me a cheater?" Triedle asked as he sank a fist into Adam's stomach.

Slocum turned him around by grabbing the gambler's arm and nearly pulling it from its socket. That way, he could look him in the eyes when he said, "You called me a liar!" Before Triedle had a chance to defend himself, Slocum punched him in the face.

Adam took that opportunity to elbow Slocum in the ribs so he could get a clear shot at Triedle. "You think all I do is sulk?"

Being a fairly successful gambler, Triedle made a living by being able to gauge a man just by observing the slightest twitch or picking up on certain tones of voice. All of those talents were either not present at the moment or being overlooked because Ed peeled back his bloodied lips to smile as he asked, "Well, isn't it?"

Since Slocum was still in front of him, Adam shoved him with all of his might so he could charge the gambler. When Slocum shoved him back, Adam responded with a backhanded swing and the two of them launched into a scrap.

"Both of you, stop it!" Mia said.

Triedle seemed to agree with her peacemaking efforts because he began slinking away from all those flailing fists. He didn't make it two steps before he was pulled into the fray and forced to defend himself.

Mia kept her distance. "Fine," she sighed. "You'll run out of steam sooner or later."

13

To Mia's surprise, the scuffle ended later rather than sooner.

All three men landed some good punches, but none were of a mind to stop swinging right away. In fact, the more hits they took, the more they wanted to deliver some of their own. When it was all said and done, the three of them looked worse than when someone had been shooting at them. The men cleaned themselves up, climbed onto their horses, with Slocum back on Mia's, and continued riding southeast along Slocum's broken trail.

To make up for lost time, they pushed the horses to a full gallop whenever the terrain would allow it. Whenever there were too many pits in the ground or rotten trees lying in their path, they slowed to navigate the obstacles and move along. Apart from the occasional notification that a watering hole had been spotted, it was a quiet ride. Once the sun had set and no town was in sight, Triedle's angry stares bored into Slocum's head. After less than an hour after sundown, however, the glow of lanterns and cooking fires could be seen in the distance. Slocum returned Triedle's gaze, snapped his reins, and rode ahead to what appeared to be more of a large camp instead of a town. He was gladder than anyone else to find the camp because, just as Triedle had accused, Slocum had made up the town as a way to spur the others into the day's ride.

The camp was centered around a small group of miners who'd pitched their tents around a bend in the Trinity River. Slocum only figured that much by observing the wooden planks hung outside the camp's trading posts and saloon. With names ranging from The Gold Pebble and Silver Strike to Fred's Turquoise Emporium, the camp was either a mining post or founded by people who had a mighty big fondness for jewelry.

Slocum steered for a large tent near the periphery of the camp that was marked by a sign that read, BUNKS FOR RENT. After he climbed down from the saddle and helped Mia do the same, he saw that neither of the other two men were following suit.

"There's another place we passed," Adam said.

"I didn't see it," Slocum replied.

"Well, it's there all the same. I'd rather sleep there." Without another word, Adam rode away.

"And I'd rather have a few drinks and maybe a game or two with some more sociable folks," Triedle said.

Slocum had already turned his back on them both so he could hitch Mia's horse to a post. "I'll stop by the saloon to collect you in the morning, but won't waste time looking under every table."

"Wouldn't expect you to." Tipping his hat to Mia, the gambler said, "If you'd rather indulge in friendly conversation, you're welcome to join me."

"No, thank you," Mia said.

"Suit yourself." Removing all of the pleasantness from his voice, Triedle added, "Good night to both of you, then."

Slocum didn't bother looking back as he stepped into the tent. It was a structure that was about the size of a small house. Heavy canvas hung on a wooden frame that sectioned the inner space into what looked to be five rooms. The first room was a narrow front area occupied by a slender woman sitting in a rocker reading a book.

"So you've decided to come in?" the woman asked.

Slocum removed his hat and wiped his brown with a bandanna. "That's right. Two rooms if you've got 'em."

"I've got four rooms, but only one is available. Do you still want it?"

Looking over to Mia, Slocum asked, "How many cots in the room?"

"Just one," the woman replied, "but I can fetch another one for a small fee."

"If there's only one cot, we're not taking the room," he told her. "So you can either fetch the cot as a courtesy to a paying customer or you can hope you get another paying customer tonight that only needs the one."

The woman sighed and pulled herself up from her chair. "You'll have the cot instead of breakfast."

Since he didn't even want to think about what sort of breakfast might be served in a hotel that was a large tent, Slocum agreed to the terms. Even then, the woman made sure to let him know how much she resented being made to leave her chair and go scrounge up another cot.

Slocum stepped outside to collect his saddlebag and hefted it over his shoulder. By the time he'd walked through the tent to find the room with the open door, the woman who ran the place was dragging a cot inside. "You'll pay up front," she shouted.

Someone from another room yelled for quiet. Slocum paid for the room, took the cot, tipped his hat, and wished her a very unheartfelt good evening. She was back in her chair, rocking and reading her book before Slocum and Mia were in their rented space.

"This really isn't so bad," Mia said.

From behind the canvas wall, the gruff voice told her

once more to shut the hell up. Slocum leaned toward that wall and spoke in a calm, even voice. "How about you get back to sleep before I light this tent on fire with you in it?"

They didn't hear the gruff voice again after that.

Mia smirked and walked over to a small trunk at the foot of the cot that had already been there. It contained a towel and a spare set of linens, which she used to get the cot ready for the evening. "This isn't bad at all," she said. "Better than outside anyway."

"I don't know about that," Slocum grumbled.

"Well, at least we don't have to bother with a fire and all." Casting a cautious glance to the wall that had spoken to her before, she dropped her voice to a whisper and said, "Maybe I should check on Adam."

Slocum tested the cot by sitting on it. Although the linens were paper-thin and the frame barely seemed capable of supporting him, he felt better than when he'd been in the saddle. "You do that."

Pausing at the door, Mia decided to shut it before leaving Slocum alone in the room. It clacked solidly as if to let her know that the tent's frame was sturdier than it appeared. "You think I shouldn't?"

"I think I'm sick of talking about him."

"Well, I guess I've just grown accustomed to the subject."

"Then I feel sorry for you. As for me, I'd rather talk about paint drying than him. You'd think with all the attention that man gets he wouldn't be so damned glum all the time."

Mia placed the sheet on the other cot and quickly got it in proper order until it looked twice as inviting as the one Slocum was on. "You're right. To be honest, it's nice to hear someone else's voice for a change."

As if on cue, the voice on the other side of the wall drifted through the air. Instead of complaining about noise, it made a loud groan, which shifted into a jarring snore. A body shifted on its cot with the creaking of old wood, dropping the snore back down to a wavering grunt.

"You don't have to put up with that when you're sleeping outside," Slocum said.

"No," Mia replied as she knelt down beside the cot. "But you also don't get any bit of privacy."

"That's what you call this?"

"Well, it's private enough for me to do this." With that, she leaned down and kissed him on the forehead. When Slocum opened his eyes, she said, "That's the first time you've done that in a long while."

"Done what?"

"Looked at me directly. Seems like you've been nothing but stern business today."

"Well, there's a job that needs to be done."

"Funny," she mused. "Today seemed like a day where the only thing we did was ride in a crooked line. I've forgotten about what we're riding toward."

"I suppose it does get that way sometimes."

"And that's something else you haven't done in a while."

"What now?" he asked.

"Smile."

Slocum reached out to place one hand on the back of her head so he could pull her forward and kiss her. The gesture wasn't necessary since she wasn't about to go anywhere, but he enjoyed the feel of her soft hair between his fingers. The touch of her lips against his was even better. They kissed a few more times, sampling the taste of each other as they came together for longer amounts of time before their mouths pressed together and their tongues slid out to brush against the other's lips.

"Oh my," she said quietly.

"Did I step over a line?"

"No, I just wasn't expecting that."

"Well, you started it," Slocum chuckled.

She smiled widely. It was brighter than the single lantern that had been provided and warmer than a stove. Her softly rounded cheeks flushed in a way to which Slocum had become familiar in the time they'd spent together. "I mean I wasn't expecting to like it quite so much," she admitted.

"Should I take that as a compliment?"

"Not just yet. Wouldn't want you to get a big head."

"Oh, is that so?"

She nodded and leaned in for another kiss. This time, she slipped her hand through his hair and immediately eased her tongue into his mouth. Slocum could feel his entire body responding to her, and before he knew it, he was pulling her onto the cot on top of him. The moment she lay down with him, the cot creaked as if it was going to give way.

"Uh-oh," he whispered. "Maybe there's another benefit to sleeping on a bedroll."

"You think this isn't strong enough for two?"

"It's barely big enough for one."

The cot creaked again, prompting them both to hop off. Slocum quickly grabbed his bedroll from the pile of his belongings in the corner and spread it on the floor. By the time he'd removed his boots, Mia had already eased out of her dress and slipped under the bedroll. She was quick enough that all he caught was a glimpse of smooth skin and supple curves before she was wrapped up again.

"Now there's something I wasn't expecting," he said.

"I'm just getting comfortable," she replied. "You can have the cot to yourself if you like."

"After all I've been through to get this far, you're not getting rid of me that easily." Slocum pulled off his clothes and climbed in with her. The bedroll was barely large enough to cover them, but that wasn't much of a concern. They were too busy running their hands over each other's bodies to worry about anything as simple as a blanket.

Mia's entire body was smooth as a peach. Her hips were round and shifted contentedly beneath his hand. When he reached around to rub the soft slope of her buttocks, she moaned softly and draped a leg over him. They were both on their sides, exploring each other while kissing passionately. When she leaned back to catch her breath, Slocum kissed a line along the side of her neck until she was almost purring like a kitten.

As they shifted beneath the blanket, Mia's hair wrapped around her face. Her limbs enveloped him, and when she felt his erection between her legs, she reached down to stroke it. Her hand moved slowly up and down along his shaft, massaging him to the point that his entire body ached. Judging by the haste with which she rolled onto her back and guided him into her, she was feeling much the same way.

She was wet and ready for him. He glided into her easily, letting out a slow breath as her tight pussy wrapped around his cock in much the same manner as her limbs wrapped around his body. "Yes," she whispered into his ear. "That feels so good."

Slocum wasn't about to argue. He was too busy savoring the feel of her naked body against him and the strength in her arms as she held him close. When he propped himself up with both arms to look down at her, Slocum took a few moments to drink in the sight of her bare breasts and hard nipples. She reached up to rub her hands along his arms, smiling contentedly as he moved in and out of her. Mia arched her back and pressed her head against the bedroll when Slocum drove in as deeply as he could go. He stayed there for a few seconds, feeling her body wrap perfectly around him.

After lowering himself all the way down onto her, Slocum wrapped his arms around Mia and kissed her again. This time, there was no playful touching of lips. There were only two people who ached to feel and taste each other with deeply probing tongues. Slocum pumped with a solid rhythm between her thighs, giving in to every thought he'd had since meeting her and enjoying the scent of her hair mingled with that of her sweaty skin.

She allowed her hands to roam freely now, grabbing his hips and massaging his naked flesh. All she needed to do was look at him for Slocum to know what she wanted. He pumped into her harder, causing Mia to clench her eyes shut and dig her fingernails into his back. Her mouth opened and closed without a single word passing her lips. The bedroll had fallen away from them, leaving them naked upon the floor. She braced her feet against the ground and spread her legs open wide so he could move freely between her trembling thighs.

Her breaths came harder now, mirroring the rhythm Slocum had built. When he drove his rigid pole all the way inside and held it there, she held on to the air in her lungs as if she expected she might not be able to catch another breath anytime soon. Slocum looked down at her, admiring the difference that had come over Mia's face since she'd given herself to him. Before, she'd been a sweet little thing with a soft voice. Now, she was grinding her hips to feel him inside her, grunting more in a voice that was akin to a low growl.

Slocum eased his hands up along her body, tracing the curves of her hips, the swell of her breasts, and finally the taut muscles of her arms. When he got to her hands, he clasped them and held them against the ground above her head. She squirmed anxiously, closing her legs as if to trap him there. When her eyes snapped open, they fixed upon him and wouldn't budge as he began pumping his cock into her with building intensity.

The wet lips of Mia's pussy tightened around him as she drew closer to her climax. After slowing his pace for a few thrusts, he pounded into her. She groaned loudly and quickly forced her mouth shut, obviously taken off guard by the pleasure that swept through her. When she arched her back and shuddered with her orgasm, Slocum could feel it in every inch of her body. That sensation, combined with the sight of her beneath him, was more than enough to push him over the edge.

He pumped into her again and again. Now that he was so close to his own climax, Slocum rocked on top of her until it came. Mia pressed her mouth against his ear so he could hear every grateful moan that she was trying so desperately to hold back.

When Slocum exploded inside her, he released his grip on her hands and practically collapsed. Before he could roll off her, she wrapped her arms around him and kissed his neck. They lay there for the better part of the night, too tired and too contented to think about using the extra cot that had been such a struggle to acquire.

14

As it turned out, missing the breakfast served in that tent was more of a punishment than Slocum had anticipated. He woke up to the smell of frying bacon, griddle cakes, and something that sent a ripple through his body that was close to the ones Mia had given him the night before.

"Is that coffee?" Slocum asked. "Real coffee?"

Mia stood at the other side of the room, easing into her dress. Even though she kept her back to him out of what seemed to be some bit of modesty, the sight of her rounded backside wriggling into her clothes was still a good one. "Yes," she said. "You think we could talk the clerk into letting us have some?"

"If it's the same lazy hag that sold us this room, I doubt it." Slocum swung his legs over the side of the cot, realizing only after his feet touched the ground that he was in a different spot than where he'd fallen asleep. "How'd I wind up here?"

"I was collecting our things and needed to pack up the bedroll. You were so tired, you didn't even open your eyes when I dragged you off of it."

119

"Damn," Slocum said while rubbing the back of his neck. "I don't remember any of that."

"You were sleeping hard. And snoring."

"Then I suppose I'd better make it up to you." He stood up, gathered up the clothes that had been piled next to the cot, and put them on. Pulling on his boots before buttoning his shirt, he opened the door and stepped through. A strong wind caused the tent's frame to creak and the walls to flap. The first thing he saw when trudging toward the front of the tent was the room directly next to his. In it, a balding man with a round belly stood with a shaving mirror in one hand and a razor in the other. He chuckled when he saw Slocum walk by and asked, "Have a good evenin'?"

"Hope we didn't make too much noise."

The man chuckled even harder and continued shaving.

Nobody was at the front of the tent, but the scent of breakfast was much stronger. Slocum walked outside through a door that was held open by a pail filled with rocks and found a trio of long tables set up next to the tent. One of the tables carried stacks of plates, piles of cutlery, and pots of coffee. A man sat behind it, wearing a dirty apron and a smile that came from the profit turned by all the customers sitting at the other two tables. Behind him, a woman stood at the opening of a smaller tent, which was filled with smoke coming from an old stove.

"Good mornin' to you!" the happy man said. "What can I get ya?"

"Some of that coffee would do nicely," Slocum said. Hooking a thumb toward the larger tent, he added, "And breakfast. I rented a room for the night if that matters."

"It sure does! Let me just double-check with my better half." He picked up a coffee cup on his way to meet with the woman at the stove. When Slocum got a look at her face as she turned around, he knew he was in trouble.

"Oh, no!" the woman said, glaring at him as if she could still feel the pains in her knees from being forced to get up from her rocker the night before. "That's the one I was telling you about. The one who made me drag that cot all the way in from the shed just so he could turn my place into a cathouse."

"I'm sure it wasn't that bad," the man in the apron said. "The least we could do is serve him breakfast. He is a paying guest, right?"

"Right and he *paid* for the extra cot instead of breakfast."

When the man looked back at him, Slocum put on the most innocent expression he could muster. It didn't do a lick of good to help his cause.

Shrugging, the man walked back to his table and filled a cup with coffee. "Apologies, mister. Help yourself to some coffee, though."

"Can I have another cup?" Slocum asked.

"One for him and one for the whore," the cranky old hag said from her stove.

"That's enough with that kind of talk, Stephie! She could be his wife, for Christ's sake!"

"He wasn't wearing no ring!"

Rather than argue the matter any further, the man shrugged and whispered, "Pay for one and I'll feed you both."

Slocum tipped his hat to him and hurried to bring Mia out before the man in the apron was forced to rescind his offer. They'd barely dug into their food before Adam staggered over to buy a plate for himself. By that time, most of the camp had gathered for breakfast. Perhaps that was why Adam didn't take notice of Slocum and Mia, but it seemed just as likely that he was ignoring them outright. Knowing he would get his fill of dealing with temperamental company throughout the rest of the day, Slocum let the matter pass so he could enjoy his meal.

As more and more of the folks at the other tables finished up and walked away, the woman who'd cooked the food started gathering up their dirty plates. When she made it to Slocum and Mia, she stopped just short of pulling the fork directly out of Slocum's hand.

"You finished?" she asked.

"Just a moment," Slocum said. He ate the eggs that had been on his fork, set it down, and handed the plate to her with a smile.

Although the woman wasn't about to grin back at him, she took the plate in the most cordial way possible. After collecting Mia's things, she stormed a few steps away and then stopped. Glancing at them over her shoulder, she said, "Someone was looking for you."

"Looking for me?" Slocum asked.

"Yes, you. Some man came around last night asking about three men traveling with a woman. I sent him on his way because there wasn't no rooms left to rent, but the description he gave matched you well enough, miss. And one of the men he described must have been you."

"Me?" Slocum asked, mostly because he didn't like having a conversation with someone's back.

"Yes," she snapped while turning around and sending one of the forks on top of her stack of plates to the ground. It landed at Slocum's feet and he picked it up before she got the chance to stoop for it. Taking it from his hand as if she thought he might bite her, the woman added, "It was you and her he described. I know because I know it was three men and a woman that rode into town and argued outside my place. I don't know who the man was that came around for you, but he wanted to find you real bad."

Slocum stood up and looked around. Although he couldn't see the entire camp, the only people he spotted were those that were wandering away with full bellies. Of course, he knew well enough that there wasn't any way for him to peer into every possible hiding spot with one glance. "The man who came asking about us, did he have long black hair and a droopy mustache?"

The woman was nodding before he even finished his

question. "And when he scratched under his hat, it looked like there was a gash along his scalp."

The only way for Slocum to get a clearer picture of Cale would be if someone actually drew one for him. "What did you say to them when they came looking for us?"

"It was right after I came back from lugging that extra cot all the way to your room. A second cot which, I might add, it sounded like you didn't even need."

"Be fair, now," Slocum said good-naturedly. "You don't know how many cots we used or didn't use."

She scowled at him, which wasn't anything new. Something that was there now that hadn't been there before was a slight hint of friendliness as she said, "From what I heard last night coming from your room, it sounded like you only needed one cot."

Unable to dispute that, Slocum let it drop.

"At any rate," she continued, "those men came along when I was cross and didn't want to do you any favors, so I told them to keep moving."

"There was more than one?" Mia asked.

"I suppose there was. Just the fellow with the long whiskers came in, but now that I think about it, there was another one or two waiting for him outside. I was mighty tired after . . . well . . . you know."

"Yeah, I know," Slocum said. He reached into his pocket for some of the money he'd won at the card table in Darnell and handed it to her. "This is for the inconvenience of dragging that cot all the way to our room, as well as the outstanding breakfast this morning. It may be a little late, but I appreciate you letting us know about the men who came looking for us."

She took the money and showed him a smile made up of a crooked, incomplete set of yellowed teeth. "You're welcome, mister. Even if we start off on the wrong foot, I like to treat my guests like they was my own kin. Were those fellas friends of yours?"

"Do you happen to know where they went?"

"They didn't tell me, but I did hear them talking."

Slocum raised his eyebrows as if he was anxiously awaiting that bit of information. The truth of the matter was that he would have been more surprised if she hadn't listened in on the conversation between Cale and his men.

"They said they'd try the Watering Hole," she told him while nodding to the second largest tent in the camp.

That was the place that Triedle had gone in search of his card game. Until that moment, Slocum had assumed the gambler was either still in his game or slumped in a chair with half a bottle of whiskey in his hand. "Have you seen any of those men since?"

"No, but I could look for them."

"That's all right," Slocum replied. "I'm sure we'll cross paths again. In fact, if they do come by your place for any reason, could you keep to your story about not knowing who we are or where we'd gone?"

"Oh, it's all right," she said quickly. "If I see them, I'll point them in the right direction. It's the least I can do after how rude I was."

"No, we'll catch up to them on our own," Slocum insisted. "And we'd like it to be a surprise." He took another few dollars from his pocket and handed them to her. "Know what I mean?"

The woman filled the blank spots in Slocum's explanation on her own. Whatever she didn't come up with, the money she'd been given made it easy enough to overlook. "Yes," she said with a wink. "I most certainly do know what you mean."

When she walked away, Slocum went over to the table where Adam was sitting. "Have you seen Ed?"

"And a very good morning to you, too," Adam grunted.

"No time for this. Have you seen him or not?"

"Nope."

"Did anyone come looking for you last night?"

"Nope."

Mia walked up to her brother and tugged at his collar to straighten it. "Where did you sleep last night?"

"No time for this either," Slocum said. "I need to find Ed before someone else does."

"Why don't I stay here with Adam?" she offered. "He can finish his breakfast and then we'll get the horses ready."

"All right, but don't dawdle."

"Yes, sir," Adam snapped. He didn't need to see any disapproving looks before he rubbed his forehead and said, "We can get everything ready just as soon as I finish eating. I'll be quick about it."

Slocum recognized the expression on Adam's face as the pained wince that marked the morning after a night of drinking. Since he already had a nursemaid to look after him, Slocum left the two siblings at the table and hurried across camp.

The Watering Hole was another tent built upon a wooden frame as opposed to the ones that had been strung up between two posts amid the leaning shacks and covered wagons that comprised the thrown-together settlement. Inside, the place looked more like something that had been set up for a church social than a saloon. The tent frame was sparse and supported by a few posts throughout its only room. A long table was situated in the back corner where drinks were served from pitchers and a crate of bottles. Round tables were scattered here and there, hosting quiet card games and a few people eating plates of beans and biscuits that looked like they'd been picked up off a desert floor. Apparently, they were the folks that couldn't afford to pay for a breakfast at the hotel.

Since Triedle wasn't to be found, Slocum walked to what he assumed was the bar and asked, "Is this the only saloon in town?"

The man behind the table wore a starched white shirt with sleeves that were neatly rolled up to his elbows. He had a kind face that shifted to an expression of surprise when he looked around and asked, "What more could you want in a saloon?"

"I'm not looking for a drink. I'm looking for a gambler named Ed Triedle. Is he here or not?"

"Sure, he's here."

"Where?"

"Right over there," the bartender said while pointing to one of the tables closest to the bar. Slocum had seen it when he'd first come in, but assumed the men sitting there quietly playing dominoes were old-timers who either lived in camp or were too put off by the noise outside to bother with a larger crowd. Something else that had made Slocum look past the table without much notice was the fact that there was no money in a pot at its center.

No matter how unlikely it seemed that he would find Triedle in such a tranquil game, Slocum approached the table. There were four men seated there, two of which were covered in silver hair or whiskers, one was bald, and the other sat peacefully with his back to the door. Slocum stepped up behind the fourth man and waited to see a reaction from any of the others. Since all he got were a few uninterested glances, he stepped to the side and looked down at the fourth man's face.

"Ed?"

Reflexively guarding his dominoes, Triedle shifted just long enough to get a look at him. "Oh, hello, John."

"What are you doing?"

"Playing dominoes. Haven't you ever seen this game? It's really quite enjoyable."

It seemed the sociable surroundings had rubbed off on the gambler because Slocum barely recognized him. In fact, even after taking a closer look, he had to wonder if he'd stumbled across someone with an uncanny resemblance to the man he knew. The bruises on his face from the previous day's scuffle told him that this was indeed the Ed Triedle he'd been looking for.

"Since when do you play dominoes?" Slocum asked.

One of the old-timers with the silver hair rapped his knuckles against the table and said, "If you want to flap yer gums, do it outside. I'm tryin' to think."

The old man had to be at least fifty pounds lighter than Slocum, was way past his prime, and unarmed. Since he was looming over the table and everyone at it with his Colt Navy in full view, Slocum couldn't help but admire the crotchety old bastard. "We're leaving," he said to Triedle. "Now."

"The hell you are!" the old-timer said. "We got . . ." He stopped to lean over so he could see past Triedle to the table where the bartender stood arranging cookies on a large platter. When he continued talking, it was in a rasping whisper. "We got good money riding on this game."

Before Slocum could say anything to that, Triedle explained, "The padre who owns this place doesn't approve of wagering."

"He'll sell liquor and allow whores in here, but doesn't want anyone to place a bet?"

"Whores?" asked the bald man. "Where?"

Triedle didn't even have to look to know what Slocum was referring to. "That woman over there isn't a whore. It's the padre's wife."

Slocum took another look at the table where two women sat eating their dry biscuits. One was a young girl in her late teens wearing a checked dress and the other was about ten years older and cinched into a dress that pushed up her breasts and put them on display within a frame of lace. "That one with the dress that don't leave much to the imagination?"

"Yep," the gambler replied. "I checked."

"Well, come on anyway. It's time to go."

The old man knocked the table once more. "Mind yer own affairs, mister. I won't tell you again."

"Keep talking, old man," Slocum snapped. "I'm not above ending the conversation in a way you won't like so much."

"Honestly, John," Triedle said. "We should respect our elders."

The old man nodded once and threw out his play. The bald man made his and Triedle was quick to lay his down to win the game.

"Son of a bitch!" the old man grunted.

Almost immediately, the bartender shouted, "Gentlemen, please! You know the rules."

"That's right," Triedle said in a soft, mocking tone. "No cursing."

Grudgingly, the other men at the table reached out to shake his hand. Each one of them slipped Triedle some money and sat back down to grumble quietly to themselves. "Now," the gambler said as he stood up and placed his hat upon his head, "you must excuse me."

"You ain't goin' nowhere," the old man said.

"You heard my friend. We have matters to tend to, but I assure you I'll be back for a rematch later. Keep my seat open."

"You can count on that."

On their way out of the saloon, Triedle nudged Slocum and said, "Didn't I tell you we make a great pair? You didn't even need any prompting and you got ol' Jeremiah riled up enough to make that boneheaded play."

"Wasn't on purpose."

"That's what makes it so brilliant! Nobody sees it coming. Not even you. Do you know how much I won in that game?"

"You mean that game run in a preacher's establishment?" Slocum asked. "A preacher that seemed like a nice enough fellow who asks that nobody gamble in his place, probably just to keep it respectable?"

"Right."

Slocum sighed, knowing he wasn't about to make a dent by trying to appeal to Triedle's sense of ethics. "How much?"

"Fifty dollars," he declared while holding the money that he'd palmed before leaving the place.

"And you say I helped distract that old-timer when he was in the middle of pondering his next move?"

"Yep. We played that whole game with me leading him to that point, and when it finally came time for him to scratch his chin and think about how to get out of the bind he was in, you came storming in there like hell in a wheelbarrow!"

"Is that a good thing?" Slocum asked.

Holding out the money one more time, Triedle replied, "I'd say so!"

"Then give me my share."

"What?"

"You just said I was a big help when you needed it. You called us a hell of a team. Isn't that the whole reason you want to come to New Orleans with me?"

"Well . . . yes, but—"

"So give me my share." When Triedle closed his fist around his winnings, Slocum said, "Doesn't bode well for a partnership if you start holding out on me. How's a team supposed to function like that?"

Triedle shook his head, peeled off a few bills, and handed them over. "You'd better make this worth it in New Orleans."

"It's a few dollars from a game of dominoes you picked up in a two-horse camp. Stop your crying."

Just as Triedle was about to defend himself, a gunshot cracked through the air. They'd walked about halfway to the tent where Slocum had spent the night, which was in the same vicinity as the gunshot. People screamed and horses thundered toward them after emerging from between a short row of wagons that had been parked nearby. Cale sat upon one of those horses and was accompanied by two of his men.

"Over here, you bastard!" Slocum shouted, trying to divert the gunman's eyes before he caught a glimpse of Adam or Mia.

Cale found Slocum right away and raised the gun in his hand so he could touch the brim of his hat with its smoking barrel. "Good mornin' to you! Just taking out a measure of the debt you owe me."

"Come over here and take it then," Slocum said as his hand lowered to within easy drawing distance of his Colt.

"I got my fill for now, but I'll be back for the rest. Don't you worry about that." He pulled the reins on his horse hard enough for it to rear up as it turned toward the east end of the camp. After that, Cale led the way out by tapping his heels against his horse's sides. Slocum fired a shot at the retreating gunmen, hoping to lure them back into the camp. The bullet sailed high over their heads but the gunmen never looked back.

"Where are you going, John?"

"To check on Mia and Adam!"

Triedle followed Slocum to the larger tent, where a crowd had once again formed. This time, it wasn't for breakfast. The people there were slowly closing in around a point near the hitching posts outside the hotel's front door. Slocum pushed his way through several stunned folks, who jumped away when he shouted at them. At the center of the crowd, Adam knelt over his sister. His hands were bloody, but the only wounds he had were from the day before. Mia lay on her side beneath the shelter Adam tried to provide with his body. Judging by the wet crimson stains on the front of her dress, she was beyond his help.

15

Mia looked up at her brother as if he was the only thing on the face of the earth. She couldn't lift her head, but didn't seem aware of the fact that she was bleeding through the fresh hole in her chest. When Slocum dropped to his knees to get closer to her, she seemed pleasantly surprised.

"Hello, John," she said.

"Mia, what happened?"

"I think I fell."

"They just rode up to us when we were getting the horses ready," Adam said. "They came out of nowhere and shouted something. When we turned around, I barely got a chance to see who was there. They aimed at her and shot." He clenched his eyes shut as tears were squeezed out from beneath his lids. "Cale shot her and rode off. I tried to get to her, but didn't move fast enough. I thought they were going to shoot me. I wanted them to shoot me. Why the hell didn't they shoot me?"

Slocum barely listened to Adam once it became clear that he didn't have any useful information. He snaked an arm under Mia's head, allowing her brother to jump to his feet and rush to his horse.

"I'm going after them," Adam said.

Without taking his eyes off her, Slocum said, "Ed, go with him."

"Right."

Without another word between them, the two men climbed into their saddles and rode away.

"I'm sorry, Mia," Slocum said.

"Sorry for what?"

"For . . ." But he couldn't bring himself to say the words. He wanted to hold her tighter, but wouldn't do that out of fear of moving her too much in her wounded state. Looking up at the crowd that was inching closer around him, he asked, "Isn't there a doctor in this damn camp?"

"There's an Army medic staying here. I can get him," a young man in the crowd offered.

"Move your ass!"

The man was already pale from witnessing the shooting, and Slocum's bellowing command hit him like a swift kick to get him running to the other end of the settlement.

Mia's hands had found the bloody spot on her chest and she tugged at the portion of her dress that was stuck to her skin. "It's starting to hurt," she whispered.

"I know, darlin'. Just be strong until the doctor gets here."

"What did you just call me?"

Slocum looked down at her. It wasn't the first time he'd noticed the warmth in her eyes or the softness of her hair, but he studied those things and so many more until they became etched into his mind. Even the faint, strained hint of a smile at the corners of her mouth was enough to reach deep inside him and make his next breath one of the most painful he'd ever taken.

"Don't worry about that," he said. "Just look at me and don't worry about what happened."

"But I think I'm hurt."

"No," he said while gently taking her hand and moving it away from her blood-soaked dress. "Don't worry about that. Just look at me."

"You're a sweet man, John. Thank you."

"Thank me later, when you have more breath."

"Thank you."

She hadn't been much of a weight in his arms, but at that moment she became almost too heavy to hold. Her head slumped down to rest against Slocum and her hand became limp in his grasp.

When Slocum looked up at the faces surrounding him, he could feel a fire blazing in his eyes. One of those faces belonged to the woman who owned the hotel and had cooked their breakfast. She was one of the few who didn't recoil from his gaze.

"You saw what happened?" he asked.

She nodded.

"The man who shot her. What did he say?"

The woman opened her mouth, only to close it again.

"Tell me!" he demanded.

"He said, a sister for a brother."

There was no reason to stay in that camp.

Adam and Triedle were able to catch sight of Cale and his men while riding after him, but it was at such a distance that they didn't have a chance to catch up to them once the gunmen reached the safety of some rocks. Adam insisted on searching the outcropping for hours, and by the time Slocum caught up to them, it was clear the killers were either gone or had dug in so deeply somewhere that they wouldn't be found unless they wanted to. Since Cale seemed intent on watching Adam suffer for a while, there was no reason to believe he would make his presence known until he was ready. If there was any silver lining to be found, that was it. Slocum wouldn't have to go looking for the murdering sons of bitches. They would come to him.

By the end of the day, Adam had said his good-byes to Mia and put her in the ground. Slocum was always amazed at how quick a funeral could be. It took a lifetime for someone to get to that point and it was over in the time it took to fill in a hole.

When they finally put the camp behind them, the sun was most of the way down. Despite the impending darkness or the fact that they probably wouldn't get far before making a camp of their own, it was more important for them to leave that place and get a little closer to where they were going. In the few hours they had to ride, none of the men looked back.

Adam would return to visit his sister's grave. That much was written in his hard-edged face and the tears he wiped away when he thought nobody was looking.

Triedle kept his mouth shut and his eyes forward, never questioning a request from the other two and never faltering when they wanted to press on.

Slocum rode with the determination of a man who would keep walking all the way to New Orleans if his horse dropped dead beneath him. Although he kept to the course that would lead him into Louisiana's port city, he no longer had his sights set upon that goal. His only concern was his next meeting with Cale. His eyes snapped toward any movement, any sound, or any other sort of hint that might tell him where those killers could be.

That night, they stopped when it became too dark to see the trail in front of them, gathered enough wood to make a fire, and huddled around it. They barely spoke.

They didn't eat.

They took turns keeping watch while the other two slept. Slocum sat facing away from the sputtering fire, his eyes slowly moving back and forth from shadow to shadow.

When Triedle approached, Slocum asked, "Why are you here?"

"I beg your pardon?"

"Surely you must know we're not riding to New Orleans to play cards after what happened."

The gambler lowered himself onto the log Slocum was using as a bench and scratched his head. "Just because we're mourning doesn't mean there aren't games to play." When Slocum glared at him, he added, "We've all lost friends and family." He cut himself off when he looked over at Adam. In the darkness, it was difficult to tell if he was sleeping or merely lying quietly with his thoughts. Rather than remind him of his most painful loss, Triedle said, "Life goes on."

"I guess I'll find myself in a saloon sometime in the future," Slocum admitted. "I'll sit down at another card game, but that's not what we're riding for. Not anymore."

"I know."

"So that brings me back around to my question. Why are you here?"

"I've been with you this far. Why wouldn't I stay for the rest?"

"Because Adam's been nothing but a pain in all of our asses and Mia was nothing to you apart from some woman who rode down the same stretch of trail for a spell. Now that this has turned bloody, why wouldn't you cut your losses and strike out on your own?"

"Why wouldn't you?" Triedle asked. This time, when Slocum scowled at him, he didn't flinch. "She wasn't your family. You knew her for as long as I did. In fact, I might have known her for longer considering I was in Bickell before you got there."

Slocum's scowl faded and he went back to studying the dark horizon.

"I'm staying to see this through," the gambler said. "I

may not be related to Mia or have had . . . other relations with her, but—"

"Wait a second. What makes you so sure there were other relations?"

"Are you telling me there weren't?"

"Well . . . no."

"It was obvious the way you two looked at each other that something else was going on between you. She fawned over you and watched you in that special way when you weren't looking."

Hearing that made Slocum feel as if he was forced to watch the light fade from her eyes one more time.

"I'm sure she's not the first woman you've been with," Triedle continued. "She's probably not the first one you've lost."

"No. She isn't."

"Well, this world can be a shit hole sometimes. Good people are killed and bastards like Cale go about their business while assholes like you, me, and that one over there keep on living. We all have to deal with our demons somehow. If you're looking for answers in that regard, I don't have any."

Whether he meant to or not, Slocum found himself looking in Adam's direction when he said, "I don't think any of us have those answers."

"If you want to know why I'm coming along for this ride," Triedle said, "that's an easy one to answer. Mia was a good woman who just wanted to help her brother. She didn't deserve to die for that or any other reason."

Slocum's gaze fixed upon some coyotes scampering after prey that was too small for him to see. "You're right about that."

Following his line of sight, Triedle leaned over and squinted until he picked out the four-legged predators. "Apart from a few coyotes, do you think there's anything out here worth finding? I know Cale and those others didn't drop off the face of the earth. Things aren't ever that simple or pleasant. I just don't know if they're close enough to get our hopes up about seeing them tonight."

"Cale did what he did for a reason," Slocum growled. "He wanted us to suffer. Wanted to light a fire under us. Spit in our faces. A man doesn't do something like that without sticking around to watch what happens afterward. He's out there, all right. He may be hiding. He may be watching. He may be keeping his head low or he may be closer than I think."

"If that's the case, maybe we should put that fire out."

"No," Slocum said as he shifted his head to look at the campfire he'd insisted on making and diligently maintaining. "I don't want him to lose sight of us. When he makes his next move, I want him to know right where to find us."

Triedle looked up as if to casually take in the sprawl of stars above him. "Or he might know right where to point a rifle and drop us like cans from a fence rail."

Slocum shook his head. "He won't do that. He's made this a dirty fight, which means he'll want to finish it up close and personal."

"Maybe he'll pick us off first and then walk in to finish it personal once we're down. Ever think of that?"

"Yeah."

"And it didn't make a dent? Am I riding with two fellows with death wishes now?"

"Remember when that fella tried to bluff you in Darnell?" Slocum asked.

"Which fella?"

"The one who had four to a flush showing when we were playing seven-card stud."

"Ah yes," Triedle said fondly. "I remember that fella."

"From the way he talked, sat, even scratched his chin, there was no reason for anyone to think he didn't have that fifth spade in his hand. If I recall, there was only one other spade showing in anyone else's hand."

"Yep."

"And you still knew he wasn't holding a fifth spade. How the hell did you pull off that trick?"

Tapping his temple with one finger, Triedle replied, "Tricks of the trade, my friend. It's all up here. Years and years of experience."

"Bullshit."

Even in the dark, Slocum could see the gambler's eyes widen. "What did you say?"

"You heard me. I said that's bullshit. If it was some sort of trick, you would have told me about it by now. Lord knows you haven't missed an opportunity to brag about every other good call you've made in the time we've spent on the trail or at meals when there was nothing else to talk about."

"And why bring this up now?"

"Because you made that call on gut instinct."

Triedle's eyes shrank back down to their normal size as he accepted the assessment with a silent shrug. "Maybe, but I don't like to rely on instinct."

"Why not?" Slocum asked. "It's some of the most accurate advice you're ever gonna get. It remembers everything you've ever lived through, it doesn't lie, and it's always there."

"It's not always accurate, though," Triedle pointed out. "There's been several calls I made on instinct that turned out to be worth less than a bag full of wooden nickels."

"That may be the case, but instinct serves you best in certain situations. The trick is knowing what situations those are. Men who can read those kinds of situations can live or die by their instinct as long as they stick to what they know. You know gambling. I know men like Cale and those killers he rides with. After what happened to Mia, my instinct is telling me that Cale is sitting somewhere laughing about how he was able to kill her and get away while we chased our tails. It also tells me he's gained enough confidence to finish the job the way he wants. That means getting his hands even dirtier and it won't be from a distance."

"I guess after what I've seen so far, I can trust your instinct."

"That doesn't mean you need to follow me for the rest," Slocum pointed out.

"Just because this world tends to throw shit our way on a regular schedule, that doesn't mean we have to like it. And we sure as hell don't have to restrain ourselves when it comes time to throw some back."

Slocum chuckled and allowed his head to hang forward. "Not exactly poetry, but I do see what you mean."

"Good. It's too damn late for poetry. Why don't you get some sleep? You've been sitting there staring at the hills for hours."

"Hasn't been that long. Has it?"

Triedle pulled the watch from his pocket, opened it, and fiddled with it to find the right angle to reflect enough moonlight on its face for him to be able to read the hands. "About an hour past the time when I was supposed to spell you."

"And just when I was starting to think you were such a good man."

"I am a very good man. Also a tired man and one who can see that you weren't in the frame of mind to be told to step aside. I figured you'd fall asleep on your own, but since that doesn't seem to be happening, I'm relieving you."

"I appreciate it," Slocum said, "but I'm fine where I am."

After the few seconds it took for Triedle to close his watch and place it back into his pocket, he set his elbows on the edges of his knees and folded his hands. "No need for us both to sit here, I suppose."

"You got that right."

"So, you might as well get some sleep because I didn't

haul my ass out of a perfectly good bedroll just to crawl back in again."

Knowing it wouldn't do any good to argue and lacking enough strength to try, Slocum walked over to the spot where he'd dropped his belongings. He used his saddle for a pillow, closed his eyes, and figured he could at least get a few minutes' rest. After a few seconds, he was out cold.

16

The next morning began for Slocum before the sun had even poked its head over the eastern slopes. The sky was just turning a warm shade of purple when he opened his eyes and pulled himself to his feet. Neither of the other two men needed much prodding before they were ready to go. In fact, the three of them stomped out the fire, got their horses saddled, and were riding without so much as a sip of coffee or a bite of breakfast. After giving their horses a chance to stretch their legs, they passed around some jerked beef and set their sights on the remainder of the day.

They rode toward the outcropping of rocks that Triedle and Adam had visited the day before when chasing Cale. As they drew closer, Adam told Slocum about what had happened when he'd followed the killers from the settlement to that spot. Unfortunately, there wasn't much to tell that Slocum couldn't have figured out on his own. Adam had been anxious to say his piece the other day, but after his sister was shot, he'd been too worked up to remember much of anything they could put to use.

"So," Slocum said after Adam finished his brief retelling of events, "you're sure this is where they went?"

"That's what I said, wasn't it? You think I'm gonna chase after the assholes that shot my sister and not be sure?"

Slocum thought about pointing out the fact that Adam had chased after them half-cocked, probably down a path that Cale had prearranged, and lost them, but decided against it. Not only would that have most likely ended up with Adam punching him in the mouth for being a smart-ass, but Slocum figured he would have earned as much for the same reason. "Where was the last place you saw them?" he asked.

Pointing toward the highest outcropping of rocks, Adam said, "They crested that hill and scattered. I tried to get after them, but couldn't find any trace of them."

"No trace at all?"

"Nope."

"How hard did you look?"

For a moment, it seemed Slocum was going to get that punch he'd avoided earlier. Then Adam realized it was an honest question and that this was no time to squabble. Grudgingly, he admitted, "When I lost sight of them, I rode a ways to the east. That's where I thought I saw some dust, but then I heard some horses that way," he said while nodding to the south. "That's when I lost them for good so I turned back."

Nodding as he surveyed the lay of the land, Slocum became certain that the killers had figured they would have some men following them and picked this as the best spot to lose them. Rather than point that out to anyone else, he announced, "We're searching these rocks, but not wasting a lot of time doing it. Have either of you men done any tracking?"

"Only things I've ever tracked down are women and suckers and only if they're inside a saloon," Triedle replied.

"Just hunting and such," Adam replied.

"Watch for scuff marks on the rocks," Slocum told them. "Anything that looks out of place and a brighter color than the rest of the rocks. We want fresh tracks or anything that shows someone's ridden through here. There was more than one of them, so the tracks should be in clumps. More than likely, they also met up again somewhere close, so I'm riding ahead. If you find something, holler. If you don't, come find me."

"What if they're hiding somewhere around here?" Adam asked.

"If you find a spot where men and horses could be hiding, let us know. Otherwise, we shouldn't waste any time looking under every rock."

Although Adam was quick to begin his search, Triedle cast nervous glances back and forth. "They shot Mia to send a message," he said to Slocum. "If they wanted to rile us up, they could be watching us right now."

"Like I said before, I'm guessing they want to finish this face to face. Even so, be on the lookout for an ambush."

"How the hell are we supposed to spot anything like that with all this damned open country?"

"I didn't say it was gonna be easy. I just said we needed to do it!"

That was more than enough to light a fire under the gambler. When Triedle rode away to search the other side of the outcropping, he didn't take his eyes away from the rocks. Slocum knew he wasn't dealing with expert trackers, but they weren't about to take the time to scour every inch. All he wanted was to find obvious tracks that might have been left behind. Adam had come up with a good point when he mentioned the killers hiding somewhere in the vicinity of those rocks. If there was a cave or gulley large enough for that, those two should be able to find it. In the meantime, Slocum had his own work to do.

He rode straight through the rocks, taking the quickest

path he could find. Along the way, he was careful to watch where he was going to make certain he wasn't trampling any of the tracks he and the other men were after. He spotted a few fresh scrapes that had been made by horseshoes chipping at the ground, but there was no way of knowing if they'd been made by Cale's men, Adam, or anyone else. Once he rode beyond the point that Adam had said he'd gone, Slocum dismounted and studied every inch of ground.

For the first fifty or sixty yards, there was nothing to see.

A few yards after that, he picked up a hint of a horse that had passed by in the last few days.

A dozen or so yards from there, things got interesting. The first set of tracks caught his eye, but only because they were the freshest ones he'd found so far. After widening the scope of his search, Slocum found another set of tracks that angled in toward the others from the south. He felt an anxious tug in his stomach, but didn't want to get his hopes up just yet. It wasn't until he found a third set of tracks joining the rest that he allowed himself to smirk.

"Nothing over there but rocks," Adam said as he rode up to where Slocum was crouched. "Damn it all to hell!"

Triedle joined them next, announcing himself with, "Sounds like you had about as much luck as I did. Still, one of you two might want to double-check because I'm no tracker."

"I heard that the first time," Slocum said. "But that's not a problem. Do either of you see what I found?"

Adam squinted at the ground for a bit before he finally jumped down from his saddle to get a closer look. Triedle, on the other hand, didn't get past the squinting part.

"What am I supposed to be seeing here?" the gambler asked.

Slocum hunkered down while shaking his head. "You really aren't a tracker, that's for sure."

"Just tell me what's got you so happy."

Too excited to wait for the other two, Adam pointed at the converging tracks and explained, "Them assholes that killed Mia scattered back there and met up right here."

"You're sure it's them?" Triedle asked.

Without hesitation, Adam replied, "Hell yes, I'm sure. Ain't that right, John?"

"We can't be absolutely sure, but it looks that way to me. The horses that left these tracks had to have passed by within the last day or two."

"I didn't see many marks like that through those rocks," Triedle said, "so that must mean that not a lot of horses came through here at all." When he looked up to find the other two staring at him, he asked, "Isn't that right?"

"We might make a tracker out of you yet," Slocum mused. "Since Adam saw those killers scatter, it only makes sense they'd regroup somewhere further along the trail. This looks like that spot."

"It sure as hell does," Adam said. "Did you find any other tracks leading away from here?"

"Not yet. Did you find anyplace in the rocks where someone could hide?"

Both of the other men shook their heads.

"Then I say we're through here," Slocum announced. "We'll follow these tracks as best we can and hope to get a jump on those murdering sons of bitches."

"I hate to be the one to spoil the party," Triedle said, "but even if we did find the right set of tracks, aren't those men still ahead of us?"

"More or less."

"And can't they still be setting up an ambush?"

"Yeah," Slocum replied, "but if we know which way they're headed, we might be able to figure a route that will allow us to get ahead of them."

"And what if they're watching us?" Triedle asked.

"Then they'll have to make their play sooner instead of

after they've had all the time in the world to lay a foundation. Either way, we're a step up from where we were before."

"Several steps up, I'd say," Triedle added. "Since you two are the trackers, perhaps I should ride out a ways to look for anyone trying to act as our shadow?"

"Think you can spot an ambush before you ride into one?" Slocum asked.

"I make a living out of knowing when someone's trying to trick me, and before you say the bleeding obvious, I've been in enough scrapes to be able to spot a fight brewing away from the card tables as well."

Slocum held up his hands and said, "Just so long as you realize what's at stake."

"I want to nail those bastards to a wall just as badly as you do." Looking to Adam, he added, "Well, maybe not as badly as you, but pretty damn bad. I'm in this until the end."

"Good," Slocum said. "Because from here on in, I won't bother to ask if you're gonna do what's necessary. If you want out, just leave when you get a chance and don't try acting friendly with me again."

"If you cut out like that," Adam said, "you'd best never cross my path either."

"Point taken," Triedle said. "Which way are we headed?"

Slocum climbed into his saddle, took another moment to study the tracks, and said, "The tracks go to the southeast. It'd be best to keep moving and cover as much ground as possible."

"I'll ride one way, circle in the other, and keep watch the whole time. Can't be as hard as spotting when that old man tried to slip those three nines past you in Bickell. I guess that's why you chose me for this chore."

"Right, Ed," Slocum replied. "Just keep rubbing those three nines in my face and I'll make sure you'll have a real hard time catching up when you want to join us for supper."

The gambler snapped his reins and rode to the east.

Adam wasn't in any mood to dawdle and he sure as

hell didn't want to joke with Slocum before following the tracks they'd found. Once they'd decided the best way to track Cale and gain ground on the gunmen, they were off and running.

17

"We got 'em on the run," Cale announced as he peered through a telescope at the trail they'd left behind.

The other two men with him breathed as if they were the ones to do all the running instead of their horses. One was a fellow wearing a battered leather vest with dozens of loops sewn across the front to hold spare rounds for the Sharps rifle he carried. His hair had thinned into a ring that encircled the back of his head from behind one ear all the way to the other. Squinting into the setting sun as if his eyes were just as powerful as any set of lenses, he said, "Looks like there's only two of them following us."

"The other one's trying to scout ahead," said the third man, who looked to be the youngest of the three. "He's been swinging back and forth between east and south all damn day."

Collapsing the telescope and dropping it into his saddle-bag, Cale said, "They're mad as hell and tearing after us like their asses were on fire. Outstanding."

"When do we take our shot at them?" the youngest one asked.

Cale looked over at him as if he'd barely said anything worth acknowledging. "Not anytime soon, Warren, so just simmer down."

The younger man gritted his teeth and ran his hand over his sweaty, pockmarked face. He was clean-shaven, but had so many scars on his chin and cheeks that it seemed doubtful any whiskers could take root there. His dark, greasy hair had the consistency of a brush that had been flattened by the dusty hat he wore. As much as he wanted to respond to Cale's scolding comment, he kept his words to himself.

Shifting his eyes to the balding man carrying the Sharps, Cale asked, "You got something to say, Bryce?"

"We shouldn't wait too long to make our move. The more time we give them, the longer they have to throw something back at us."

"You knew my brother, right?"

"Yeah. He was a good kid."

"The way he was killed don't call for some half-assed potshots being thrown at the ones that gunned him down. The job needs to be done right, not just quick."

"I know that," Bryce said. "But we can't take too long to do it."

"Let me ask you something else. Do you know who it is that killed my brother?"

"John Slocum," Warren said as if he was expecting a prize. "I heard of him."

Cale turned to face the youngest member of the group as if he'd only popped into existence. "Really? And what have you heard?"

"I heard he took on a gang of rustlers outside of El Paso."

"Make that two gangs of rustlers," Cale corrected. "And he did it single-handed."

"He bushwhacked most of 'em," Bryce said. "And it wasn't El Paso. It was Santa Fe."

"Odds are that both of you are right," Cale said to his

men. "John Slocum's spilled more blood than a guillotine and there's probably plenty more that we don't even know about."

"A what?" Warren asked.

"A guillotine. Didn't you ever read a goddamned book?"

Judging by the offense he took from that comment, it seemed Cale's words had definitely struck a nerve. Warren grumbled to himself and then turned toward the south. "Are we headed into town or not? The more we stand around gossiping, the more time we give to them assholes."

"He's right," Bryce said. "We knocked them off their guard and managed to get away before they came after us when we killed that woman. No need to let them get any closer to us. A man don't have to be John Slocum to make good on mistakes like that."

"We ain't made a mistake yet," Cale snarled. "But we gotta make them think we did. That's why two of us will be moving along like we're happy as pigs in slop and the third will be keeping an eye on Slocum, Adam, and that other one."

"You don't think they'll notice they're only following two of us?"

"Not if we get far enough ahead of them. And if we can't get ahead of a bunch like that, we deserve to get caught. What's the closest town from here?"

Both of the others thought about it, but Warren was first to answer. "Adalee is less than a day's ride southeast," he said.

"What's farther than that?"

"What about Teaghan's Cross?" Bryce offered. "If we ride like bats out of hell, we should be able to make it there by tomorrow morning. Even sooner if you want to ride through the night."

"No need to push it that hard," Cale said. "We just need to put some distance between us, give ourselves a chance to run Adam Weyland and Slocum in circles for a while and tire them out before letting them get somewhere they can rest. More than likely, they'll tucker out before getting to town."

Snapping his fingers, Warren said, "We may even get them to think we're holed up in Adalee! It's a small town, but they might waste the better part of a day searching it from top to bottom if they think we're there."

Cale nodded. "That ain't such a bad idea. In fact, since you're so fired up to go there, you should be the one to lead them to that spot. Be sure to stay there for a while to be certain they take the bait. In fact, you might wanna let them catch sight of you so they're sure to follow you into Flattery."

"Not Flattery. Adalee."

"I don't give a shit if the town's painted red and called Hell," Cale said. "Just make sure them assholes see you go there and stay for a while so we can set something up proper in Teaghan's Cross."

"And how do you propose I lead them to the next town?" Warren asked. "Let them shoot at me for a few miles?"

"More than just a few miles," Bryce said. "You might want to make sure your horse is good and rested before you strike out from Adalee."

Before the younger gunman could say what was on his mind, Cale told him, "If they're good enough trackers to get to Adalee, they'll make it to Teaghan's Cross. It ain't like we're gonna hide or make it too tough for them."

"That's fine for you to say," Warren groused. "You ain't the one acting like a clay pigeon in a shooting gallery."

"I swear to Christ, you whine more than that bitch we killed. You've been talking so tough about how well you can handle yourself and how bad you wanted to prove yourself by collecting on this debt but now you turn your nose up at leading three cocksuckers around by the nose?"

"One of those cocksuckers is out to kill the men who put his sister in the ground and another is a known gun hand!"

"You know who else is a known gun hand?" Cale asked while drawing his pistol and aiming at a spot directly between the younger man's eyes. "Me! Do your fucking job before I cut the deadweight from this outfit right here and now."

To his credit, Warren didn't flinch when that gun was pointed at him. He merely grit his teeth and forced himself to nod as he said, "All right, Cale. No need to get rough with me."

"Are you gonna lead those men where we want them to go, or should we waste even more time jabbering about it?"

"I said I would, didn't I?"

"Not so's I'd believe it."

That seemed to have a greater impact on the younger man than the pistol that was being pointed at him. Setting his jaw into a stoic grimace, he said, "I'll do it."

Cale nodded and lowered the gun. When he spoke again, it barely caused his drooping mustache to shift. "Now I believe you. Get the hell out of my sight."

Warren steered his horse away from the men that Cale had spotted through his telescope and flicked his reins to get the animal moving slowly away. Only after there was no chance of showing himself to the men they were hunting did he get moving any faster than that. And only after he'd put plenty of distance between him and his two partners was another word spoken.

"That might not have been a good idea," Bryce said.

"Why not? This is my outfit, ain't it?"

"Yeah, but we're a little out of our range here. All the time I've known you, we've lent money to men too stupid to know any better and knocked some heads around when they didn't pay up. Back in Amarillo, we had a proper gang. This may be more than we can chew."

"What about the Forcelli brothers? We cut one of 'em up so the other could watch. And when he didn't pay us, we cut him next so we could help ourselves to all the livestock they bought with the money they borrowed. Was that more than you could chew?"

"First of all, going after a man like John Slocum ain't anything like going after a pair of no-good leeches like the Forcellis. Them brothers shot their mouths off and got what was coming to them. Slocum is something else. He's dangerous."

"So are we," Cale quickly reminded him. "And when word spreads that we collected our debt even when someone like him was trying to keep us from it, we'll be able to write our ticket in Bickell as well as that whole county and at least three others. We might be able to pull together a better gang than we ever had before."

"You think we can take him?"

"Yeah. A reputation ain't nothing but talk. Even if some of them stories about him are true, that just means he can use a gun. So can we. Hell, you can pick them off while they're riding from a hundred yards away."

"Then why the hell haven't you let me do that yet?" Bryce asked.

"Because my brother deserves better."

Those words were spoken with such ferocity that Bryce didn't dare question them. Every muscle in Cale's body was tensed, which meant he was just as ready to pull the trigger of his gun now as he'd been when it had been aimed at Warren. Rather than push the matter any further, Bryce let it rest.

Shifting his gaze to the path in the distance, Bryce squinted and studied the men riding it. "Still haven't found that third man. There's only two down there."

"You know your arithmetic," Cale chuckled. "That puts you several notches above Warren."

"The other one could have spotted us by now."

"If he had, them other two wouldn't be moseying along the way they are. Don't you agree?"

"I suppose, but that doesn't mean we should stay here much longer."

"If we're going to convince them that we're still together, we need to lay down tracks they won't miss. The fresher the better. As long as we stay close together and ride in single file, Adam or them others won't be able to tell if they're following two or three men."

"An experienced tracker would know," Bryce pointed out.

"That's why I sent Warren out ahead of us. He's sure to be spotted, which means he'll lead them in the right direction. And since he'll be spotted on his own, an experienced tracker will just assume he's the scout and that they picked up the remaining trails when they find ours. As soon as we hit Adalee, we split up to break off our tracks and then you ride ahead to Teaghan's Cross."

"What will you be doing?"

"Hanging back to provide a few more bread crumbs for them to follow."

"Ain't that the kid's job?"

"Sure," Cale replied. "But Warren may get himself killed along the way. If he don't, he'll just make things even more confusing for Adam and his two partners until they find their way to where we want them to be. Since Slocum's such a bad man, let's give him a proper target to shoot at."

"What if they're watching us closer than we think?"

"Then they'll just see two of us headed into Adalee. If you're not good enough to get to where you're going, then you—"

"I know," Bryce cut in. "I deserve whatever I get. Why didn't you tell Warren about the rest of this plan before sending him away?"

"Because he's the weakest link in this chain. There ain't no reason to confide in a weak link. How much time do you need in Teaghan's Cross before the rest of us show up?"

Bryce scratched his chin as he led his horse farther away from the ridge. By the time he climbed into his saddle, he'd arrived at his conclusion. "A full day would be best. That'd allow me to get a feel for the town and clear a few paths to set up a reception for Slocum and Adam. What about the third man? Do you know anything about him?"

"Name's Ed Triedle. Just some two-bit gambler who makes a living cheating ranch hands and cowpokes out of their salary."

"Is that all?"

"As far as I'm concerned," Cale said while settling into his saddle and riding to the northeast, "once my brother was shot dead, every last one of those assholes became the same thing in my eyes. Dead. First I killed that bitch sister of Adam's and now I run them other three until they're too tired to see straight. After that, I don't care if Adam's got John Slocum, Wild Bill, or the devil himself riding alongside him. They'll all be dead."

18

ADALEE, TEXAS

Slocum followed the tracks from the outcropping of rocks, only to realize they'd circled completely back around to a ridge overlooking the trail he'd ridden earlier that day. It didn't take a very big leap in logic to figure out Cale and his men had been watching them throughout the day and had moved on long before they were in danger of being discovered. From there, he'd picked up three sets of tracks that all pointed him toward a meandering trail that ended at another small town. This one was larger than a camp, but not by much. It consisted of three streets that were wide enough to accommodate a stagecoach and several smaller avenues that were barely suitable for walking. Along all of those routes were shops, homes, a schoolhouse, two churches, and three saloons.

"Well," Triedle mused, "at least they got their priorities straight."

"If you intend on looking for a game in one of those saloons, you might as well stay there."

"That's not what I meant, John. Aw, hell. If you don't trust me by now, it ain't gonna happen. All I know is that I'm sick of explaining myself to the likes of you."

Slocum nodded and swung down from his saddle so he could lead his horse to a livery. "I can understand that. Consider the matter dropped."

That was all that was said on the subject, but it was plain enough to tell by the tone in his voice that Slocum would drop a fist or his boot on some delicate portions of the gambler's anatomy if the trust he'd been given was proven to be misplaced.

Once the horses were tended, both men walked along the town's main street. "So them tracks led here?" Triedle asked.

"That's right. Adam swore by it and the ones I found didn't make me think otherwise."

"You think they're still trying to keep watch on us?"

"Oh, I know they are."

That stopped Triedle as surely as if a door had been slammed in his face. "How can you be so certain of that?"

"We've said that all along. Weren't you listening?"

"Sure, but you sound like you're talking about the sun coming up tomorrow. Like it's not an educated guess."

"It's not. I saw one of them riding alongside our trail outside of town."

"You think he was watching us or just riding in to town?" Triedle asked.

"Probably both." When Triedle fixed a concerned glare on him, Slocum asked, "Why does that surprise you?"

"Because you never mentioned that you actually spotted someone. I mean, we knew they could be watching us, but that we would just be keeping an eye out."

"Obviously you were doing a bang-up job there," Slocum chuckled. "Besides, you were too worked up about getting picked off by a rifle. If I would have said something about being followed, you would have just gotten yourself whipped up into a lather."

"I think that's something worth fretting about!" Looking around as if he was surprised by the tone of his own voice, Triedle lowered it when he asked, "Where did our shadow go?"

"I don't know. I lost sight of him about a mile outside of town."

"What?"

"Which is another reason why I didn't mention it."

Triedle sighed and put his back to the wall next to the front door of a saloon. "Is this some twisted way of paying me back for all that New Orleans talk?"

"Yeah," Slocum admitted. "A little bit."

"So what now?"

"I'll look through this town and you'll ask about any strangers."

"Brilliant," Triedle said. "So I just step right up to a bar and ask if anyone's seen any killers lurking about? That should work just fine so long as Cale and his boys were announcing who they are and what they're doing."

"I said look for strangers, smart-ass. If there's one thing any barkeep knows, it's when strangers come to town. If they don't know, there are plenty of others in those places who would. You know," Slocum added as he cast a sideways glance at Triedle, "unsavory types like yourself."

"Never pass up a chance to sneak in a jab, do you?"

"Not if I can help it."

"Fine. I'll ply my trade while you do what? Look for cathouses?"

"Just do your job so we can get the hell out of here and move on if that's what we need to do."

Triedle grumbled to himself while storming into the saloon. By the time he was through the front door, he was already waving and greeting the locals as if he'd spent his entire life in that town.

19

Warren stood in the cramped little room, leaning toward the window and staring down at the street. One hand was lost in a bunch of curtains that he'd gathered up and moved away from the glass so he could peek outside. The other was clenched around the grip of his .45 and couldn't seem to decide whether the pistol should stay holstered or come out to play.

His eyes narrowed as his upper lip curled back in response to the sight below. He watched as Slocum and Triedle eventually met and then parted ways on the street below. After the gambler went to the saloon, Slocum nearly got himself trampled by a wagon in his haste to cross the street. Since Warren wasn't sure how much the other men knew about what was going on, he was ready to do anything from fire out the window or jump through it as the fastest means to get to ground level.

"What do you want here?" the woman behind him asked.

Without taking his eyes from the window, he snapped, "Shut yer mouth, bitch!"

She didn't seem rattled by the gruff tone of his voice, but obviously didn't appreciate it either. "If all you want is a view of the street, then—"

"I told you to shut yer damn mouth!" Warren said as he drew his gun and turned to aim it at her.

The woman in the room with him was about a foot shorter than Warren and wasn't shocked by his display of temper in the slightest. In fact, she moved toward him as if drawn to the gun in his hand. "No reason for all of that, honey. I'm just saying there's plenty more in this room than just the window."

Although there was still some anger in his eyes, Warren didn't know quite what to make of her. Rather than make more of a ruckus than what was necessary, he grumbled, "Sorry about that."

Her hair flowed well past her shoulders in a thick, golden wave. Her rounded cheeks were colored by a little bit of rouge, but her lips didn't need any help whatsoever. They were a natural red and curled into a seductive smile as she stepped up and placed her fingers on the barrel of his gun. "Think you could put that away for now?"

"Yeah," Warren said as he holstered the .45 and spun around to look out the window. "Just leave me alone. I'm busy."

Not to be deterred so easily, she came up behind him and slid her arms around his torso while pressing against his back. "Too busy for me? You sure about that?"

Warren's eyes drooped shut as he savored the touch of her hands against his chest. He snapped them open again and forced himself to keep his attention focused on the street. "I'm sure."

"If we don't conduct some business of our own," she whispered, "Jersey will send some of his boys to kick you out of here. You can't just charge through the front door, shove your way upstairs, and hole up in a room that anyone else would have to pay for."

"Who the hell is Jersey?"

"The man who runs this establishment and he doesn't mind cleaning blood off his floors."

Despite the hesitation in his voice, Warren put on his bravest snarl when he said, "He can send all the men he wants up here. If he interrupts me before I'm ready to go, I'll kill them all."

"Or we could just conduct our own business." She eased one hand down along his stomach and cupped his groin as she added, "It'd be a whole lot better than fighting."

Warren's erection grew no matter how hard he tried to keep his mind on the task at hand. She massaged him expertly, shifting between vigorous strokes and slow caresses. When he caught sight of Ed Triedle stepping out of the saloon, he let out a relieved sigh.

"What do you say?" she asked. "Ready for that business or would you still rather watch?"

"Just give me a minute."

"Another minute and your business will be done, sugar. Then you'll owe me some money."

More horses ambled down the street, and when they passed, the gambler crossed to meet with his partner. Triedle had plenty to say and gestured with his arms in all directions, but Slocum remained calm. He placed his hands on his hips, kept his back to the hotel, his gaze on the far end of town, and finally started walking toward the livery.

The woman's hands stopped where they were, holding Warren's rigid pole as if she hadn't decided whether to keep petting it or to tear it off. "I followed you up here before Jersey could send anyone to kick you out. If you're trying to keep watch for someone, just tell me and I can put the word out. It'll cost a bit extra, but I know damn near everyone in town."

"Don't need any help with that," Warren said.

"Then how about you take advantage of my hospitality?"

"You a whore?"

"Like to think of myself as a hostess," she replied. "A hostess who likes men and don't see a problem with getting paid to do what I do best."

"Thought this was a boardinghouse or maybe a hotel."

"Either way, you'd need to pay for a room. At least here you'll get a little something extra."

"Why should I pay for it?"

"Because what I got is too good to give away for free."

Outside, Slocum and Triedle were on their horses and riding down the street. Warren tried to get a better look at them, but could only see their silhouettes surrounded by the dust kicked up by their horses. Once they reached the corner, they snapped their reins and took off as if they'd been shot from a cannon. Warren smirked at the sight of them scampering away like rabbits.

"So what will it be?" she asked. "You gonna pay to keep Jersey happy or for me to keep you happy?"

"What's your name?"

"You can call me Belle."

Once Slocum and Triedle had ridden out of his sight, Warren turned around to face her. Belle's eyes were light blue and became wide with the surprise of his sudden movement. When she started to take a step back, he grabbed hold of her wrist and said, "Maybe you should've let sleeping dogs lie, Belle. I'm not just any sort of man who can be trifled with."

"Is that so?"

"Hell yes, it is. I'm an honest-to-God killer. What do you think of that?"

When he'd said that sort of thing to the girls in the town where he'd grown up or folks who stepped out of line after meeting him on the street, he always sparked a bit of fear that made the effort worthwhile. Belle, on the other hand, didn't even try to pull her wrist from his grasp.

"I think that's the reason I came up here," she said. "You look like you know how to use that gun of yours."

"I know how to use it, all right."

Leaning so her full, rounded breasts touched his chest, she dropped her voice to a hungry whisper and said, "Then stop talking and use it."

Warren shoved her toward the bed and started unbuckling his belt. Now that there was nothing worth watching in the street, he didn't give a damn what was happening on the other side of the window. Fortunately, Belle was giving him plenty to look at.

Although she hadn't been shoved that hard, she staggered back until her legs hit the bed. Then she dropped down onto it and propped one foot against the side of the mattress so her skirts fell away to reveal a smooth, creamy leg. She smiled as if she got a thrill from sliding her hand along her thigh. "That's it," she purred. "Take out that gun."

He couldn't get his boots and shirt off fast enough. Rather than kick his pants off, he lowered himself on top of her the moment they were around his ankles. His gun belt hit the floor with a noisy thud that he barely seemed to notice. When Warren groped between Belle's legs, he discovered she wasn't wearing anything beneath her dress. Her pussy was warm and wet, covered with a thick patch of downy hair.

Spreading her legs a bit more, she wriggled beneath him until they were lying on the middle of the mattress. As soon as she felt his rigid pole brushing against her, she drew a long, deep breath. "What are you waiting for?" she demanded. "Put that in me and get to work."

He wasn't quick enough. Warren soon felt her hand wrap around his erection and guide it straight to her moist opening. After pumping into her once, that same hand grabbed him by the waist and pulled him closer while she bucked against him. It wasn't until he was thrusting hard enough to make the bed creak that he finally got a reaction out of her.

"Harder!" she cried.

Despite what he might say to Cale or anyone else while

sitting around a campfire, Warren hadn't been with many women. Belle was the first that not only became excited by a rough manner, but couldn't get enough of it. The harder he pumped into her, the wetter she got. Finally, he allowed himself to give in all the way and pound into her with every bit of strength he had.

At the first sign of him letting up, Belle gripped his arms and moved her hips with a rhythm of her own. When she pressed her hands flat against his chest, he didn't have the will or the strength to resist. Belle flipped him onto his back and climbed on top of him. Fixing her eyes upon him while reaching between his legs, she said, "We're not through yet, cowboy."

For the first time in his life, Warren was speechless with a woman. Her grip was so firm as she grabbed his cock that he was afraid to move. Within seconds, she lowered herself onto him and eased her wet pussy all the way down to the base of his shaft. Belle braced both hands against his chest and arched her back as she rode him. Every muscle in her body strained and she tossed her blond hair back while hitting her stride.

"Go on," she moaned. "Tell me what a bad man you are."

Warren couldn't catch a deep enough breath to form the words.

"Call me a whore."

No matter how good she felt, he simply couldn't figure out how to react. Finally, it seemed the only thing he could do was what he was being told.

"Come on, whore," he said unconvincingly. "Is that all you got?"

She smiled without opening her eyes to look at him. Her hips bucked even harder and she rode his cock as if she was angry at him for a wrong he'd committed. When Warren stirred beneath her, she leaned with all of her weight resting on the palms of her hands to hold him down. Warren held on to her hips, which was like trying to wrangle a wild bronco without the benefit of a rope.

After ripping open his shirt, Belle moved her hands to his stomach. She straightened to sit almost perfectly upright on top of him. Her hips weren't moving as quickly, but had taken to thrusting in shorter, stronger motions. When he started breathing heavier, Belle slapped her hands against his bare skin and said, "You better not think you're done yet, boy."

Warren didn't like being called that no matter who was doing the talking. He tried to sit up and put her in her place, but Belle shoved his back flat upon the mattress and then ground her hips in a slow circle. The easier pace and smooth glide of her pussy along his cock took the fire from his eyes. After lowering herself down so he was as far inside her as he could get, she wriggled her hips back and forth until her eyelids began to flutter.

"That's the spot," she sighed.

In all the times he'd been with a woman, he'd never seen one look as blissful as when Belle pulled in a sharp breath and pumped her hips one more time. Her pussy tightened around him and her next exhale turned into a lingering laugh. "Now," she said while easing off him, "it's your turn."

From Warren's perspective, it seemed as if Belle had slid down between his legs and completely off the bed. Her hands remained on his chest and moved along the front of his body to come to a rest on his legs. When he sat up, he could see that she was kneeling on the floor beside the bed. She smiled up at him while tugging his legs to get him to scoot closer to her. As soon as he'd gone far enough, she took hold of his cock and wrapped her lips around its tip.

Her mouth was warm and wet as it enveloped him. She moaned softly while easing her head down, and when she moved it up, she let her tongue graze along the bottom of his shaft. Very quickly, she picked up her pace until her head was bobbing between his legs. Her tongue moved so fast that he could barely tell what it was doing. She was making him feel so good, however, that Warren just leaned back and enjoyed himself.

Belle's hands moved up and down along his hips and then stretched up to rub his stomach. As she sucked him, her hair brushed his skin to add another layer of sensation to what was already rolling through him. Once he'd caught his breath, Warren reached down to place both hands on the back of her head and guide her as he pleased.

In stark contrast to how she'd been earlier, Belle responded to every one of his unspoken requests. When he wanted her to go faster, she sucked him hard enough to make his toes curl. And when he wanted her to stay still, she kept her head in place as he pumped into her mouth. As soon as he drew a single breath that was sharper than the others, she took the reins back.

Placing her hands on his hips, she grabbed hold and held on tight as she sucked him. Her fingernails raked against his skin as her mouth worked vigorously. All the while, she moved him back until he was once more lying in the middle of the bed. She crawled on top of him like a predatory cat, licking his legs, thighs, stomach, and penis. Although Warren had wanted to direct her again, he quickly found it was better to let her do her work. She licked his cock like it was the tastiest stick of candy ever made, and when she moaned softly while he was still in her mouth, the pleasure was too much to bear.

He felt his knees go weak and his shoulders rise up from the mattress as he exploded in her mouth. Belle kept her lips wrapped around him, moaning softly until he was too spent to stay upright. After letting him fall from her mouth, she gave him a gentle shove, which was more than enough to drop him to his back on the bed.

"Sweet mother of God," he moaned.

"Aren't you glad you paid for that instead of dealing with Jersey just to look out a window?"

"Y-Yes."

"Now, about that payment."

As he lay there, Warren felt the room spinning. When he closed his eyes, he swore he could feel not only the room but the entire world turning beneath him. Belle placed her hand on his chest and tapped him insistently, but he wasn't about to open his eyes and break the peaceful spell he was under.

"Get out of here," Belle said.

Judging by the creak of the door hinges and floorboards, Warren knew she wasn't talking to him. It looked like he would get to meet Jersey after all. Fortunately, he was feeling good enough to take that bull by the horns. He snapped his eyes open, craned his neck, and looked at the door.

Instead of some grumbling brothel owner, Warren saw Slocum looking down at him over the top of his Navy Colt.

"You heard the woman," Slocum said. "Maybe it's time we talked about payment."

20

Warren rolled onto his side and then sat up so he could get to where his gun belt was piled on the floor near the back of the room. In the time it took for him to pull up his britches, Slocum had already stormed inside, circled around the bed, and cut him off.

"How'd you find me?" Warren asked. "I saw you leave!"

"You've been following us and we've been following you," Slocum replied. "The tracks were a bit harder to follow once they reached this town, but it wasn't impossible. Some folks in a saloon told my partner there was a gunman holed up here and I circled back to have a look. Any more lessons in manhunting will cost you more than you already owe."

"I don't owe you anything!" Warren growled.

Slocum snapped a quick jab into Warren's face and said, "There's where you're wrong."

Already off balance, Warren flopped over the foot of the bed and slid off to land on all fours upon the dusty floor. When he hopped up, the first thing he saw was Belle with her legs curled against her chest and her shoulders pressed against the headboard doing her best to stay out of the fracas.

By the time Warren turned in Slocum's direction, another punch was headed his way. It caught him in the jaw to snap his head to one side and send him straight down again. When the room spun around him this time, it wasn't such a good thing.

"The way I see it," Slocum said, "you owe me for all the trouble you've caused. Until you and your asshole partners came along, I just wanted to finish a job in New Orleans."

Warren was getting tired of being knocked around. The frustration showed on his face even better than if it had been painted on him in bright colors. He did his best to get up while backing away, but that only caused him to stagger like a drunk into the chest of drawers against the wall. "Nobody asked you to do a damn thing."

Slocum stayed on the other side of the bed. "True. To be honest, I barely even recall what the hell my job was supposed to be in New Orleans. See what a nuisance you are?"

Turning toward Belle, Warren asked, "Where the hell is this Jersey fella you were going on about?"

"If you mean the big man who owns this place," Slocum said, "he's still downstairs. Your name's Belle?"

"Yes," she said.

"That big man said you should go before you got hurt."

Taking only a moment to look at Warren, she pulled her skirts down and climbed off the bed on the side that was closest to the door. She stopped short of the door, turned back around, and said, "You still owe me for the tumble we took."

"How much money are you carrying?" Slocum asked.

Still trying to hike up his britches, Warren sputtered, "Are you joking?"

"From where I stand, she provided a service and you took it. Isn't that right?"

"It sure as hell is," Belle said.

Slocum was smirking at the younger man, but since he was doing it over a Colt Navy, he was making a good impact. Warren grumbled to himself, dug through his pockets, and threw some cash across the room.

"Don't make me force you to pick that up," Slocum warned.

But Belle had already stooped to collect it and seemed pleased with what she'd found. "It's all right. There's plenty here to cover what he owes."

"You sure about that?"

She nodded enthusiastically. "And then some."

"A gratuity on top of the fee," Slocum mused. "Very civil. You'd best get out of here, ma'am. Do me a favor and make sure we're not bothered for a little bit."

Warren's hopes for Jersey to be his guardian angel were dashed when she said, "That won't be a problem. He just paid for the room for the next hour."

Slocum nodded and circled around the bed to meet the younger man. "Very civil indeed." After Belle had left and shut the door tightly behind her, he dropped his voice to something close to a growl and said, "Tell me where Cale is headed."

"What the hell do you care? He ain't after you."

"Funny, but those shots that were fired at me tell a much different story."

"He's after Adam Weyland."

"It's gone well beyond that," Slocum replied. "You saw to that when you killed Mia Weyland for no good reason other than to prove a point."

Warren couldn't figure out how to dispute that. Rather than try to talk his way out of the room, he began plotting to shoot his way out. Slocum deduced that much when the young man's eyes darted toward the gun belt lying on the floor.

"You want to jump for that pistol?" Slocum asked. "It's so close, you could probably get to it before I hit you."

"You'd gun me down before I was even armed," Warren spat.

"You think so?"

"Probably the only way you could take me on. Probably the way you killed most of the men everyone says you killed. Back-shooting son of a bitch, sneaking in on me when I'm dipping my wick."

Slocum raised an eyebrow. "You've got a point there. Shooting an unarmed man does seem a might on the cowardly side."

"It sure does."

"What about shooting an unarmed woman? How's that sit with you?"

Once again, Warren was at a loss for words.

Narrowing his eyes in a way that completely erased the easygoing manner he'd taken a moment ago, Slocum asked, "When Mia was killed, was she armed? And before you try to lie to me, you little piece of shit, remember that I'd been riding with her every step of the way since we left her house."

"No, she wasn't armed. It wasn't me that shot her, though."

"Who was it?"

"Cale," Warren said without hesitation. "And he'd be the one to tell you that to your face if you bothered looking him in the eye."

"I'm not the one that's been running away before we get close enough for that meeting. Also, if you inch toward that gun one more time, I'll drop you where you stand."

Frustrated that he hadn't been able to get any farther than a quarter of an inch toward his gun belt, Warren angrily stood up straight and pulled his jeans up. "Cale's not even here!"

"Where'd he go?"

"I don't even know. He's got a big enough lead on you by now that he could have changed course ten times already."

"But he's not looking to throw us off his trail, is he?"

"Fine," Warren snapped. "He's headed across the border to the first town in Louisiana you'll find along the trail out of here. Some little piss hole I never even heard of."

"There's plenty of towns, camps, and whatnot between here and the border. And there's more than one trail that leads from here to Louisiana."

Warren flapped his hands in front of him and let out an exasperated breath. "I don't know what the hell you want from me, Slocum. First you ask where Cale is headed, and when I tell you, all you can do is give me more hell for it!"

"That's because I don't want the answer that Cale wants me to hear."

"What's that supposed to mean?"

Slocum kicked the bed with enough force to make it skid across the floor and knock into Warren's shins. "Don't give me that bullshit! You think you're smarter than me, boy? You think you can feed me whatever you want and I'll just swallow it down? Even the woman that just left this room would know better than that."

Warren was unable to disguise the tremor in his voice when he asked, "What do you want to know?"

Silence filled the room like smoke until it became thick enough to cause a choking fit. "Maybe," Slocum said in a cold tone that slithered through that smoke like a snake through shallow water, "I've been spending too much time with gamblers and card cheats. Something tells me you wouldn't give me the truth right now even if your life depended on it, which I can guarantee you it does."

"I know about you. I know how many men you killed."

"You don't know a goddamn thing about me, kid," Slocum growled.

Holding up his hands as if that would be enough to protect himself, Warren said, "I know you're not just talking. I know my life depends on telling you the truth, so that's what I'm doing."

"No. You're a tough-talking little asshole who thinks he's got things rattling around in his head that us lesser men have never thought of before. All you're trying to do is buy time until you can get to that gun. That's why you've slid your stinking little foot another inch closer to it just now."

No matter how futile the gesture was, Warren pulled his foot back.

"Tell you what, kid. You want a fair shot at me? You got it." With that, Slocum turned his pistol sideways, opened his hand, and let it drop to the bed. It hit the blanket with a muffled thud, bounced once, and lay still. "Now we've both got to make a reach for our guns. That fair enough for you or do I have to drop my britches around my ankles?"

Warren's face showed every bit of the anger that boiled inside him. His lips curled into a twisted line as he struggled to choke back one insult after another. Finally, when he looked down at the gun that Slocum had dropped, he decided he didn't need to choke any longer. Rather than go the direction he'd been pointed, Warren lunged for Slocum's Colt instead of dropping down for the .45 wrapped up in his own holster on the floor.

Using the same speed he would have utilized to grab his Colt from its holster, Slocum snapped his hand down to grab Warren by the wrist. From there, all it took was a quick twist and a pull to grind the younger man's hand against its joint and shove him away from the bed. Slocum reached for his Colt and got to it, but didn't get a chance to turn around before Warren was attacking him.

Favoring the hand that hadn't been twisted the wrong way, Warren punched Slocum's ribs in a desperate barrage. All Slocum could do was drive his elbow around and turn his body before any bones were broken. The elbow glanced off Warren's arm and was followed by a clubbing blow from the Colt that thumped against his shoulder. When he twisted around to try and shield his head, Warren left his ribs open for a few chopping punches that stole the breath from his lungs.

Hearing Warren's wheezing gasps, Slocum knew he had a chance to land a few more blows before the kid got some more wind in his sails. He delivered a clean uppercut to Warren's jaw, which sent him back to land on the edge of the bed. Rather than approach him there, Slocum dug his toe under the mattress and kicked it and Warren off the frame. By the time they hit the floor, Slocum had walked around to meet him.

"Tell me where the ambush is being set," Slocum said. "And don't give me any bullshit about a town in Louisiana."

"That's all I got for you. I swear!"

Since that story had been the first thing out of Warren's mouth, Slocum knew it was the one that Cale wanted fed to him. Also, the kid had given it up too easily. That suited him just fine since beating on the younger man for a little while longer wasn't an unattractive prospect.

One edge of the mattress was trapped beneath Warren and the other curled around him like the shell of a burrito. Slocum placed his boot onto the mattress and stomped the younger man as if he intended on knocking him through the floor. Even with the extra padding, he could tell his boots were making an impact.

"Stop it!" Warren shouted in a voice that was muffled by the mattress. "Let me catch my breath."

Slocum squatted down and pushed the barrel of his Colt against the upper edge of the overturned mattress. "What've you got to say to me, Warren?"

"I swear! That town I told you about is—"

The thump of Slocum's Colt cut him off as it sent its round into the mattress and out the other side amid a flurry of stuffing and feathers. "What was that about Louisiana?" he asked.

"I wasn't lying about—"

The Colt barked again, this time punching a hole through

the mattress that was close enough to Warren for him to feel its passing.

"Better reconsider quickly," Slocum warned. "This mattress is about to burn."

If Warren thought that was a bluff, he guessed again when he caught a whiff of burning material coming from the little fire that had been started by the gunshots.

Slocum watched the flames grow, ready to stomp them out if necessary, but not wanting to do it too soon. "The fire's spreading," he said. "I bet you'll start to squeal once it gets to you."

Warren kicked and flailed to get out from where he was trapped, only to be knocked back into place by Slocum's boot. Slocum kept stomping until he'd put out the small fire and held the younger man in place still wrapped up in the dirty mattress.

"Think I'll just let you burn," Slocum bluffed. "Serves you right for what happened to Mia."

"No, no! It's Teaghan's Cross!"

Slocum took his foot off the mattress and stepped back so Warren could find his own way out. When the younger man flopped away from the bed and rolled until he bumped against the door, Slocum was right there waiting for him with his Colt held in place.

"Teaghan's Cross?" Slocum asked.

"That's the town you want. Cale's tracks were gonna lead you through it on your way to the Louisiana border and that first place I told you about."

Everything from the desperate tone in Warren's voice to the speed with which he spat out his words told Slocum that he was telling the truth. He may not be completely trustworthy, but he was too panicked to lie convincingly. "Where is it?"

Warren rattled off some directions while anxiously patting at his clothes and kicking at the mattress as if he and it were both engulfed in flames.

Slocum listened to every word and was too busy working out the details in his head to enjoy the sight in front of him. "What were you supposed to do here?"

"Keep an eye on you and make sure you were headed in the right direction. After you left, I was gonna catch up after giving you a head start and then keep you following me for as long as I could."

"Following you all the way to Teaghan's Cross?"

There was just enough shame in his eyes to be convincing when Warren nodded and said, "Yeah."

"Good. Now there's still the matter of what happened to Mia."

"I told you, I didn't have anything to do with killing that bitch."

"I'm glad you put it that way, kid."

Propping himself up, Warren got his legs situated so he could climb back to his feet. "You are?"

"Yes," Slocum said while stooping to collect Warren's .45. "I am." He tossed the gun over the bed so it landed upon the mattress, which now lay flat between the frame and the door. "You've been a big help. For that, I'll hand you over to the law and be done with it. Seems fair, doesn't it?"

Warren studied him carefully. "I suppose it does."

Slocum holstered his Colt and turned so his left shoulder faced the window. Looking over while peeling back the curtains, he was treated to the same view of the street that Warren had been utilizing not so long ago. "Now I just need to figure out where the sheriff's office is, or if this town even has a sheriff."

With Slocum gazing out the window and his gun lying within reach, Warren took advantage of the situation he'd been given. He didn't stop to think that Slocum had given him that path willingly, which meant he was surprised when Slocum responded at the first sign of movement.

Warren managed to get his gun in hand before Slocum drew his Colt and extended his right arm. By the time the younger man brought his gun up to fire, Slocum had already pulled his trigger. The Colt Navy bucked once against his palm, drilled a hole through Warren's heart, and sent him crashing against the door. The kid's body slid down and flopped right back onto the mattress he'd tried so hard to escape.

There was some commotion outside and Slocum intended on leaving, but then an idea drifted through his head. After sizing up the dead man on the floor, he smirked and began searching the rest of the room. He found a battered jacket and hat resting on a chair, both of which fit him well enough to suit his needs.

On his way out of the brothel, he passed a portly man, who took up a good portion of the hallway leading to a staircase. Slocum walked past him and said, "Sorry about the mess," while handing him a few more dollars of the poker money he'd won.

"What was that shooting?" the fat man demanded. "Was anyone hurt?"

"Just a kid with a big mouth who tried to kill me," Slocum replied. "I'm leaving my horse and a pair of saddlebags. Sell them off to cover any damages or just to make up for your trouble."

That seemed to take most of the concern from Jersey's face. "You know his name in case anyone asks?"

"Don't worry about it. Nobody will ask."

21

TEAGHAN'S CROSS

Cale only had to wait a day for Warren to arrive. He caught sight of the young man as he rode into town amid the thunder of hooves and a cloud of dust that had been kicked up by them. Recognizing the horse as well as the basic silhouette of the man riding it, he stepped away from the Pump and Pail Corral while holding up his hand to shield his eyes from the sun. Before he could shout out a single word of greeting, the rider turned in his saddle and pointed behind him at another group of horses coming in to town.

"You couldn't have gotten here any earlier?" Cale shouted as he raced into the stable where his horse and saddlebags were being kept.

Warren galloped by without even looking in his direction and circled the stable while reining his horse to a stop.

"Goddamn kid," Cale grumbled.

"What's the matter?" Bryce asked from another stall.

"Warren just arrived and he's got Slocum and them others hot on his heels."

Bryce stood up and dusted himself off. His bedroll was spread out on one side of the stall, where he'd been sleeping. "Should I get ready for them?"

"No, you ignorant shit. Just stand there and kick straw at them when they get here!"

Shaking his head while collecting his rifle, Bryce slapped his hat onto his head and jumped over the gate of the stall he'd rented. As soon as the horses thundered past the front of the corral, he pushed open a door and ran across the street along the path he'd scouted upon his arrival. In no time at all, he'd circled around to the back of the dry goods store across from the Pump and Pail.

Cale checked to make sure the shotgun he'd grabbed was loaded before propping it against a post a few paces away from the stable's main doors. He was checking the ammunition in his pistol when Warren strode around the corner with his head lowered. "Did they see you come in here, kid?" When he didn't get an answer right away, Cale turned toward the man approaching him. Although their builds were similar, the hat and jacket were the same, and the horse had been the one that Warren had stolen outside of Bickell, the man wasn't Warren.

"Hello there," Slocum said.

In a flicker of motion, Cale extended his arm and fired a quick shot. The bullet knocked a hole into the wall several feet away from its target, but bought him enough time to fling himself through the door and into the stable. "Didn't think you'd make it this far, Slocum!"

Slocum wasn't about to answer the gunman's taunting voice. Doing that would only waste the element of surprise he'd worked so hard to acquire by impersonating a dead man long enough to get close to his target without springing the trap that had been set for him. At this point, all that mattered was that Slocum held Cale's attention long enough for the rest of the plan to fall into place.

Drawing his Colt, Slocum fired a high shot through the

door that was guaranteed to do nothing more than make a lot of noise. Fortunately, he didn't have to waste another bullet before Triedle came along to provide an even bigger distraction.

The gambler traced his steps back up the street, firing into the air and scattering the locals, who didn't have the first notion of what was going on. Those shots, along with a few screams and shouts from him and those frightened townspeople, made more than enough noise to cover Slocum's footsteps as he circled around to the back of the stable.

"All we wanted was Adam!" Cale shouted while firing through the door. "But you'll make a damn fine bonus! I was even gonna offer you a cut of the profit if you handed him over, Slocum. Too late now!"

Cale fired again through the door before he kicked it open. Outside, there was nothing but dust swirling in the air.

"You're right," Slocum said while entering the stable through the back door. "It's too late to set this straight the easy way."

Grinning wide, Cale reached for the shotgun he'd placed by the door. As soon as he felt its weight in his hands, he pointed it at Slocum and pulled the trigger.

Slocum was just fast enough to dive to the floor as the scattergun went off. He heard several pieces of buckshot chew into the stalls around him as splinters filled the air like gritty wooden rain. Scrambling to get his feet beneath him, he raced to the closest stall and jumped into it as Cale's second shot ripped through the air. Since that emptied both of the shotgun's barrels, Slocum stood up to fire a shot of his own but the gunman was already bolting outside through the front door.

"Come out and face me like a man!" Cale shouted. "Or are you too yellow to do anything more than to trick me by wearing another man's hat?"

"If that's all it took to fool you," Slocum said while heading for the door, "then I wouldn't be so loud about it."

Cale stepped into the street while drawing his pistol. Upon seeing Triedle, he immediately shifted his aim to fire a few shots at the gambler. They hissed close enough to their target to force Triedle to steer away from the corral for the shelter provided by some neighboring buildings. While taking a few quick glances up toward the roof of the dry goods store, Cale reloaded.

No more than a second passed after Slocum stepped out of the stable before a rifle shot cracked through the air. Cale smiled victoriously while looking at the store's roof one more time. Since he couldn't see anyone up there even after another shot was fired, the joy on his face was replaced with confusion.

"You're not the only one who can send scouts ahead," Slocum declared. "For some reason, Adam had all the patience in the world when it came to tracking you down and hiding in the shadows until the time came to blow your head off your shoulders. And guess what. That time has come."

Still confused, Cale watched the dry goods store until Adam staggered out from the alley between it and its neighbor. He gripped his side and winced with every step. "I got him, John!"

"You'd best have my money, too, you son of a bitch!" Cale snarled. "Along with the deed to that land!"

"Give it up, Cale!" Slocum shouted. "This has gone far enough already."

Cale didn't throw up his hands. He didn't even make Slocum wait before turning around to raise his pistol and take aim.

Slocum beat him to the punch with a quick shot that clipped Cale's hip and knocked him down as surely as a kick from a mule.

"No!" Adam shouted before Slocum could fire again. "He killed my sister! I want to finish him off!"

Before Slocum could talk any sense into him, Adam pulled his trigger. Like any other wounded animal, Cale fought without regard for his own well-being. Now that he wasn't hampered by the worry of getting shot, he took no notice of Adam's weapon while firing at him. The next shot came from farther down the street and blasted out a piece of Cale's left shoulder. The impact knocked him to the dirt, but the gunman insisted on pulling himself up again.

Slocum reflexively turned toward the source of that last shot, finding Triedle walking down the street with his rifle to his shoulder. He levered in another round, shifted his aim, and fired at Bryce, who'd attempted to circle around the dry goods store to get behind Slocum. Judging by the bloody wound in his ribs, Bryce had been too hurt to climb up to the store's roof. Now, thanks to Triedle's shot, he wasn't about to go anywhere. He dropped to his knees, but still tried to fire his rifle. Triedle talked him out of that with one more shot from his rifle that punched a hole through Bryce's skull.

Adam's pistol went off next. That round caught Cale high in the chest and sent him back down in a heap. Standing over him, Adam looked at the gunman as if he couldn't believe his own two eyes. "Get up, you bastard!"

Slocum approached Adam, aiming his gun at Cale but knowing fairly quickly that such precautions weren't necessary. "It's over," he said while holstering his pistol. "He's dead."

"No. It's not over."

"He's dead, Adam! See for yourself."

Adam's dark blond hair was filthy and tussled. His eyes were wide as saucers and his mouth fumbled for more words. He held his breath while looking down at Cale, only to let it out in an anguished wail as the gunman's body slackened and expelled its final breath.

"See?" Slocum said. "It's over."

"What happens to me now?"

"Don't worry about that. All these folks here saw these men taking shots at us. Hell, someone here probably knows they've been here waiting to bushwhack us over some debt."

Suddenly, Adam's gun was raised and pointing at Slocum's face. "I'm not talking about that," he snarled. "I'm talking about what happens when I become sicker and fade away."

Looking down at the bloody spot in Adam's side, Slocum said, "You're wounded. Isn't that enough of your blood spilled in one day?"

"That asshole tried to stick me with his knife," Adam replied. "It's not enough to do the job."

"What job, Adam?"

"I won't shrivel up like my ma did! I won't curl into a fucking husk in some sickbed!"

"Still after your ticket off this earth?"

"Gentlemen?" Triedle said as he stepped forward. "Perhaps we should get something to eat. We've still got a ride ahead of us."

Slocum silenced him with a backward wave and then squared his shoulders to Adam. "You're sick. Plenty of folks are sick. You're dying. We're all dying. You're also a man. Bite the bullet and take what this world gives you just like the rest of us."

"Fuck you, Slocum. I'm not dying. I'm already dead!" With that, he extended his arm and glared at him over the top of his old .44. "I just ain't in my grave yet."

Even with that gun pointed at him, Slocum didn't budge. "You did a good job here. You came along with your sister when she asked. You even set things straight with these murdering dogs when she was killed. Plenty of men wouldn't have the sand to come as far as you have."

"I'm too tired to go any further."

"We're all tired. I'm no doctor, but you sure as hell aren't a ghost. You're alive and that means you got more to do before moving on to whatever's next."

"Are you spouting religion to me, John?"

Slocum had to chuckle at that. "If there was a cause to hang a man for hypocrisy, that would be it. I'm just telling you to do your sister's memory proud and live the rest of your life with honor."

The fire in Adam's eyes gave way to pain.

The pain gave way to sadness.

After that, Adam could no longer hold his gun up. His arm hung loosely from his shoulder and he winced at the pain from the wound in his side that he'd overlooked until that moment. "I think I need to see a doctor," he said while grabbing the bloody portion of his shirt.

Slocum took the gun from him and looped Adam's arm across the back of his shoulder so he could help support his weight. "Yeah. I've been told you're feeling a little sick?"

When Adam laughed, he winced even harder. "That man with the rifle didn't have what it took to kill me."

"That's right," Triedle said as he rushed up to them. "God saves up all the best luck for idiots and fools. Any more of Cale's men left?"

"If there were, they've skinned out of here," Slocum said. "Now make yourself useful and find a doctor to help dress this wound."

The gambler moved around to support Adam's other side. "We're still going to New Orleans, right?"

"Not me," Adam said. "I've got a home to get back to."

"Right, but before that we're going to New Orleans? I mean, we came this far!"

"Ed," Slocum grunted, "you're right." When Triedle's face brightened, he added, "God does heap good luck onto idiots. If I didn't have my hands full right now, you'd be flat on your back with a busted nose."

Watch for

SLOCUM AND THE BANDIT CUCARACHA

388th novel in the exciting SLOCUM series
from Jove

Coming in June!

DON'T MISS A YEAR OF

Slocum Giant
by
Jake Logan

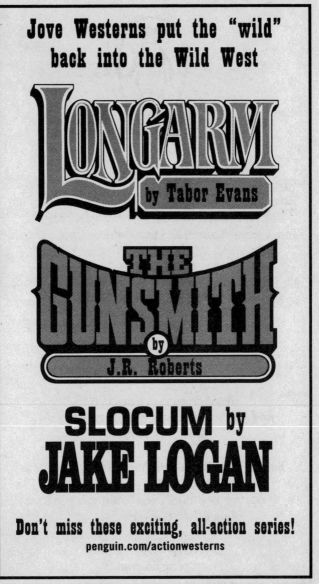